JANE

PASTE JEWELS

Being Seven Tales of Domestic Woe

BY

JOHN KENDRICK BANGS

"They also serve who only stand and wait"

NEW YORK AND LONDON
HARPER & BROTHERS PUBLISHERS
1897

TO

E. L. N.

PREFACE

It may interest the readers of this collection of tales, if there should be any such, to know that the incidents upon which the stories are based are unfortunately wholly truthful. They have one and all come under the author's observation during the past ten years, and with the exception of "Mr. Bradley's Jewel," concerning whom it is expressly stated that she was employed through lack of other available material, not one of the servants herein made famous or infamous, as the case may be, was employed except upon presentation of references written by responsible persons that could properly have been given only to domestics of the most sterling character. It is this last fact that points the moral of the tales here presented, if it does not adorn them.

J. K. B.

YONKERS, N. Y., 1897.

CONTENTS

THE EMANCIPATION OF THADDEUS

THE EMANCIPATION OF THADDEUS

THEY were very young, and possibly too amiable. Thaddeus was but twenty-four and Bessie twenty-two when they twain, made one, walked down the middle aisle of St. Peter's together.

Everybody remarked how amiable she looked even then ; not that a bride on her way out of church should look unamiable, of course, but we all know how brides do look, as a rule, on such occasions—looks difficult of analysis, but strangely suggestive of determined timidity, if there can be such a quality expressed in the human face. It is the natural expression of one who knows that she has taken the most important step of her life, and, on turning to face those who have been bidden to witness the ceremony, observes

that the sacredness of the occasion is
somewhat marred by the presence in
church of the unbidden curiosity-seek-
ers, who have come for much the same
reason as that which prompts them to
go to the theatre—to enjoy the spec-
tacle.   But Bessie's face showed nothing
but that intense amiability for which she
had all her life long been noted ; and as
for Thaddeus, he never ceased to smile
from the moment he turned and faced
the congregation until the carriage door
closed upon him and his bride, and then,
of course, he had to, his lips being otherwise engaged.   Indeed, Thaddeus's amiability was his greatest vice.   He had never been known to be ill-natured in his
life but once, and that was during the
week that Bessie had kept him in suspense while she was making up her mind
not to say "No" to an important proposition he had made—a proposition, by-the-
way, which resulted in this very ceremony,
and was largely responsible for the trials
and tribulations which followed.

Thaddeus was rich—that is, he had an income and a vocation ; a charming little home was awaiting their coming, off in a convenient suburb ; and, best of all, Bessie was an accomplished house-keeper, having studied under the best mistresses of that art to be found in the country. And even if she had not completely mastered the art of keeping house, Thaddeus was confident that all would go well with them, for their waitress was a jewel, inherited from Bessie's mother, and the cook, though somewhat advanced in years, was beyond cavil, having been known to the family of Thaddeus for a longer period than Thaddeus himself had been. The only uncertain quantity in the household was Norah, the up-stairs girl, who was not only new, but auburn-haired and of Celtic extraction.

Under such circumstances did the young couple start in life, and many there were who looked upon them with envy. At first, of course, the household did not run as smoothly as it might have done—meals

were late, and served with less ceremony
than either liked ; but, as Bessie said, as
she and Thaddeus were finishing their
breakfast one morning, " What could you
expect ?"

To which Thaddeus, with his customary
smile, replied : " What, indeed ! We get
along much better than I really thought
we should with old Ellen."

Old Ellen was the cook, and she had
been known to Thaddeus as " Old Ellen "
even before his lips were able to utter the
words.

"Ellen has her ways, and Jane has
hers," said Bessie. " After Jane has
got accustomed to Ellen's way of getting
breakfast ready, she will know better how
to go about her own work. I think, perhaps, cook's manner is a little harsh. She
made Jane cry about the omelet this
morning; but Jane is teary, anyhow."

" It wouldn't do to have Ellen oily
and Jane watery," Thaddeus answered.
" They'd mix worse than ever then. We're
in pretty good luck as it is."

"I think so, too, Teddy," Bessie replied; "but Jane is so foolish. She might have known better than to send the square platter down to Ellen for an omelet, when the omelet was five times as long as it was broad."

"You always had square omelets, though, at your house — that is, whenever I was there you had," said Thaddeus. "And I suppose Jane's notion is that as things happened under your mother's régime, so they ought to happen here."

"Possibly that was her notion," replied Bessie; "but, then, in your family the omelets were oblong, and Ellen is too old to depart from her traditions. Old people get set in their ways, and as long as results are satisfactory, we ought not to be captious about methods."

"No, indeed, we shouldn't," smiled Thaddeus; "but I don't want you to give in to Ellen to too great an extent, my dear. This is your home, and not my mother's, and your ways must be the ways of the house."

"Ellen is all right," returned Bessie, "and I am so delighted to have her, because, you know, Teddy dear, she knows what you like even better, perhaps, than I do — naturally so, having grown up in your family."

"Reverse that, my dear. Our family grew up on Ellen. She set the culinary pace at home. Mother always let her have her own way, and it may be she is a little spoiled."

"Do you know, Teddy, I wonder that, having had Ellen for so many years, your mother was willing to give her up."

"Oh, I can explain that," Thaddeus answered. "I'm the youngest, you know; the rest of the family were old enough to be weaned. Besides, father was getting old, and he had a notion that the comforts of a hotel were preferable to the discomforts of house-keeping. Father likes to eat meals at all hours, and the annunciator system of hotel life, by which you can summon anything in an instant, from a shower-bath to a feast of terrapin, was

rather pleasing to him. He was always
an admirer of the tales of the genii, and
he regards the electric button in a well-
appointed hotel as the nearest approach
to the famous Aladdin lamp known to
science. You press the button, and your
genii do the rest."

"But a hotel isn't home," said Bessie.

"A hotel isn't this home," answered
Thaddeus. "Love in a cottage for me; but,
Bessie, perhaps you—perhaps it wouldn't
be a bad idea for you to speak to Jane
and Ellen this morning about their differences. I am an hour late now."

Then Thaddeus kissed Bessie, and went
down to business.

On Thaddeus's departure Bessie's cheer-
fulness also deserted her, and for the first
time in her life she felt that it would do
her good if she could fly out at somebody
—somebody, however, who was not endear-
ed to the heart of Thaddeus, or too inti-
mately related to her own family, which
left no one but Norah upon whom to
vent the displeasure that she felt. Norah

was, therefore, sought out, and requested
rather peremptorily to say how long it had
been since she had dusted the parlor;
to which Norah was able truthfully to
answer, "This mornin', mim." Whereupon Bessie's desire to be disagreeable
departed, and saying that Norah could
now clean the second-story front-room
windows, she withdrew to her own snug
sewing-room until luncheon should be
served. She was just a trifle put out with
Norah for being so efficient. There is
nothing so affronting to a young house-
keeper as the discovery that the inherited family jewels, upon whom much reli-
ance has been placed, are as paste along-
side of the newly acquired bauble from
whom little was expected. It was almost
unkind in Norah, Bessie thought, to be
so impeccably conscientious when Jane
and Ellen were developing eccentricities;
but there was the consoling thought that
when they had all been together a month
or two longer, their eccentricities would
so shape themselves that they would

fit into one another, and ultimately bind
the little domestic structure more firmly
together.

"Perhaps if I let them alone," Bessie
said to herself, "they'll forget their differences more quickly. I guess, on the
whole, I will say nothing about it."

That night, when Thaddeus came home,
the first thing he said to his wife was:
"Well, I suppose you were awfully firm
this morning, eh? Went down into the
kitchen and roared like a little tyrant,
eh? I really was afraid to read the paper
on the way home. Didn't know but what
I'd read of a 'Horrid Accident in High
Life. Mrs. Thaddeus Perkins's Endeavor
to Maintain Discipline in the Household
Results Fatally. Two Old Family Servants Instantly Killed, and Three of the
Kitchen Table Legs Broken by a Domestic Explosion!'"

"Be serious, Thaddeus," said Bessie.

And Thaddeus became instantly serious. "They—they haven't left us, have
they?" he whispered, in an awe-struck tone.

"No. I—I thought I'd let them fight it out between themselves," replied Bessie. "You see, Thaddeus, servants are queer, and do not like to have their differences settled by others than themselves. It'll work out all right, if we let them alone."

"I don't know but that you are right," said Thaddeus, after a few moments of thought. "They're both sensible girls, and capable of fighting their own battles. Let's have dinner. I'm hungry as a bear."

It was half-past six o'clock, and the usual hour for dinner. At 8.10 dinner was served. The intervening time was consumed by Jane and Ellen endeavoring to settle their differences by the silent, sniffy method—that is, Jane would sniff, and Ellen would be silent; and then Ellen would sniff, and Jane would be silent. As for Thaddeus and Bessie, they were amused rather than angry to have the dear little broiled chicken Bessie had provided served on the large beef-platter; and when the pease came up in a cut-glass

salad - dish, Thaddeus laughed outright,
but Bessie's eyes grew moist. It was too
evident that Jane and Ellen were not
on speaking terms, and there was strong
need for some one to break the ice. Fortunately, Bessie's mother called that evening, and some of her time was spent
below - stairs. What she said there only
Ellen and Jane knew, but it had its effect,
and for two or three weeks the jewels
worked almost as satisfactorily as did
Norah, the new girl, and quite harmo-
niously.

" Bessie," said Thaddeus, one night as
they ate their supper, " does it occur to
you that the roast is a little overdone to-
night ?"

" Yes, Teddy, it is very much over-
done. I must speak to Ellen about it.
She is a little careless about some things.
I've told her several times that you like
your beef rare."

" Well, I'd tell her again. Constant
dropping of water on its surface will
wear away a stone, and I think, perhaps,

the constant dropping of an idea on a
cook's head may wear away some of the
thickest parts of that—at least, until it is
worn thin enough for the idea to get
through to where her brain ought to be.
You might say to her, too, that for several nights past dinner has been cold."

"I'll speak to her in the morning," was
Bessie's reply ; and the dear little woman
was true to her purpose.

"She explained about the beef and the
cold dinner, Ted," she said, when Thaddeus came home that afternoon.

"Satisfactorily to all hands, I hope ?"
said Thaddeus, with his usual smile.

"Yes, perfectly.   In fact, I wonder we
hadn't thought of it ourselves.   In the
old home, you know, the dinner-hour was
six o'clock, while here it is half-past six."

"What has that got to do with it ?"
asked Thaddeus.

"How obtuse of you, Teddy !" ex-
claimed Bessie. " Don't you see, the poor
old thing has been so used to six-o'clock
dinners that she has everything ready for

us at six ? And if we are half an hour late, of course things get cold ; or if they are kept in the oven, as was the case with the beef last night, they are apt to be over-done ?"

" Why, of course. Ha ! Ha ! Wonder I didn't think of that," laughed Thad-deus, though his mirth did seem a lit-tle forced. " But—she's—she's going to change, I suppose ?"

" She said she'd try," Bessie replied. " She was really so very nice about it, I hadn't the heart to scold her."

" I'm glad," was all Thaddeus said, and during the rest of the meal he was silent. Once or twice he seemed on the verge of saying something, but apparently changed his mind.

" Are you tired to-night, dear ?" said Bessie, as the dessert was served.

" No. Why ?" said Thaddeus, shortly.

" Oh, nothing. I thought you seemed a little so," Bessie answered. " You mustn't work too hard down-town."

" No, my dear girl," he said. " I won't,

and I don't. I was thinking all through
dinner about those girls down-stairs. Perhaps—perhaps I had better talk to them,
eh ? You are so awfully kind-hearted,
and it does seem to me as though they
imposed a little on you, that's all. The
salad to-night was atrocious. It should
have been kept on the ice, instead of
which it comes to the table looking like a
last year's bouquet."

Bessie's eyes grew watery. " I'm afraid
it was my fault," she said. " I ought to
have looked after the salad myself. I always did at home. I suppose Jane got it
out expecting me to prepare it."

" Oh, well, never mind," said Thaddeus, desirous of soothing the troubled
soul of his wife. " I wouldn't have men-
tioned it, only Jane does too much thinking, in a thoughtless way, anyhow. Servants aren't paid to think."

" I'll tell you what, Thaddeus," said
Bessie, her spirits returning, " we are
just as much to blame as they are ; we've
taken too much for granted, and so have

they. Suppose we spend the evening
putting together a set of rules for the
management of the house ? It will be
lots of fun, and perhaps it will do the
girls good. They ought to understand
that while our parents have had their
ways—and reasonable ways—there is no
reason why we should not have our ways."

"In other words," said Thaddeus,
"what we want to draw up is a sort of
Declaration of Independence."

"That's it, exactly," Bessie replied.

"Better get a slate and write them on
that," suggested Thaddeus, with a broad
grin. "Then we can rub out whatever
Jane and Ellen don't like."

"I hate you when you are sarcastic,"
said Bessie, with a pout, and then she
ran for her pad and pencil.

The evening was passed as she had suggested, and when they retired that night
the house of Perkins was provided with
a constitution and by-laws.

"I don't suppose I shall recognize my
surroundings when I get back home to-

night," said Thaddeus, when he waked up in the morning.

"Why not?" asked Bessie. "What strange transformation is there to be?"

"The discipline will be so strict," answered Thaddeus. "I presume you will put those rules of ours into operation right away?"

"I have been thinking about that," said Bessie, after a moment. "You see, Thad, there are a great many things about running a house that neither you nor I are familiar with yet, and it seems to me that maybe we'd better wait a little while before we impose these rules on the girls; it would be awkward to have to make changes afterwards, you know."

"There is something in that," said Thaddeus; "but, after all, not so much as you seem to think. All rules have exceptions. I've no doubt that the cook will take exception to most of them."

"That's what I'm afraid of, and as she's so old I kind of feel as if I ought to respect her feelings a little more than we

would Norah's, for instance. I can just
tell you I shall make Norah stand around."

"I think it would be a good plan if you
did," said Thaddeus. "I'm afraid Norah
will die if you don't. She works too hard
to be a real servant—real servants stand
around so much, you know."

"Don't be flippant, Thaddeus. This is
a very serious matter. Norah is a good
girl, as you say. She works so much and
so quickly that she really makes me tired,
and I'm constantly oppressed with the
thought that she may get through with
whatever she is doing before I can think
of something else to occupy her time.
But with her we need have none of the
feeling that we have with Jane and Ellen.
She is young, and susceptible to new im-
pressions. She can fall in with new rules,
while the other two might chafe under
them. Now, I say we wait until we find
out if we cannot let well enough alone,
and not raise discord in our home."

"There never was an Eden without its
serpent," sighed Thaddeus. "I don't ex-

actly like the idea of fitting our rules to
their idiosyncrasies."

"It isn't that, dear. I don't want that,
either ; but neither do we wish to unnec-
essarily hamper them in their work by de-
manding that they shall do it our way."

"Oh, well, you are the President of
this Republic," said Thaddeus. "You
run matters to suit yourself, and I believe
we'll have the most prosperous institution
in the world before we know it. If it
were a business matter, I'd have those
rules or die ; but I suppose you can't run
a house as you would a business concern.
I guess you are right. Keep the rules a
week. Why not submit 'em to your mother first ?"

"I thought of that," said Bessie. "But
then it occurred to me that as Ellen had
served always under your mother, it would
be better if we consulted her."

"I don't," said Thaddeus. "She'd be
sure to tell you not to have any rules,
or, if she didn't, she would advise you
to consult with the cook in the matter,

which would result in Ellen's becoming
President, and you and I taxpayers. She
used to run our old house, and now see
the consequences !"

" What are the consequences ?" asked
Bessie.

" Mother and father have been driven
into a hotel, and the children have all
been married."

" That's awful," laughed Bessie.

And so the rules were filed away for
future reference. That they would have
remained on file for an indefinite period
if Thaddeus had not asked a friend to
spend a few weeks with him, I do not
doubt. Bessie grew daily more mistrust-
ful of their value, and Thaddeus himself
preferred the comfort of a quiet though
somewhat irregular mode of living to the
turmoil likely to follow the imposition
of obnoxious regulations upon the aris-
tocrats below-stairs. But the coming of
Thaddeus's friend made a difference.

The friend was an elderly man, with
a business and a system. He was a man,

for instance, who all his life had break-
fasted at seven, lunched at one, and dined
at six - thirty, of which Thaddeus was
aware when he invited him to make his
suburban home his headquarters while
his own house was being renovated and
his family abroad. Thaddeus was also
aware that the breakfast and dinner hours
under Bessie's régime were nominally those
of his friend, and so he was able to assure
Mr. Liscomb that his coming would in
no way disturb the usual serenity of the
domestic pond. The trusting friend came.
Breakfast number one was served fifteen
minutes after the hour, and for the first
time in ten years Mr. Liscomb was late in
arriving at his office. He had not quite
recovered from the chagrin consequent
upon his tardiness when that evening he
sat down to dinner at Thaddeus's house,
served an hour and ten minutes late, Ellen having been summoned by wire to
town to buy a pair of shoes for one of her
sister's children, the sister herself suffering from poverty and toothache.

" I hope you were not delayed serious-
ly this morning, Mr. Liscomb," said Bessie, after dinner.

" Oh no, not at all !" returned Liscomb,
polite enough to tell an untruth, although
its opposite was also a part of his system.

" Ellen must be more prompt with
breakfast,"said Thaddeus. "Seven, sharp,
is the hour.   Did you speak to her about
it ?"

" No, but I intend to," answered Bessie.   " I'll tell her the first thing after
breakfast to - morrow.   I meant to have
spoken about it to-day, but when I got
down-stairs she had gone out."

" Was it her day out ?"

" No ; but her sister is sick, and she
was sent for.   It was all right.   She left
word where she was going with Jane."

" That was very considerate of her,"
said Liscomb, politely.

" Yes," said Bessie.   " Ellen's a splendid woman."

Later on in the evening, about half-
past nine, when Mr. Liscomb, wearied

with the excitement of the first irregular
day he had known from boyhood, retired,
Thaddeus took occasion to say :

" Bessie, I think you'd better tell Ellen about having breakfast promptly in
the morning to-night, before we go to
bed."

" Very well," returned Bessie, " I'll go
down now and do it ;" and down she
went. In a moment she was back. "The
poor thing was so tired," she said, "that
she went to bed as soon as dinner was
cooked, so I couldn't tell her."

" Why didn't you send up word to her
by Jane ?"

" Oh, she *must* be asleep by this time !"

" Oh !" said Thaddeus.

It was nine o'clock the next morning
when Ellen opened her eyes. Breakfast
had been served a half-hour earlier, Jane
and Bessie having cooked some eggs,
which Bessie ate alone, since Thaddeus
and Liscomb were compelled to take the
eight-o'clock train to town, hungry and
forlorn. Liscomb was very good-natured

about it to Thaddeus, but his book-keeper
had a woful tale to tell of his employer's
irritability when he returned home that
night.   As for Thaddeus, he spoke his
mind very plainly — to Liscomb.   Bessie
never knew what he said, nor did any of
the servants; but he said it to Liscomb,
and, as Liscomb remarked later, he seemed
like somebody else altogether while speaking, he was so fierce and determined about
it all.   That night a telegram came from
Liscomb, saying that he had been unex-
pectedly delayed, and that, as there were
several matters requiring his attention at
his own home, he thought he would not
be up again until Sunday.

Bessie was relieved, and Thaddeus was
mad.

"We *must* have those rules," he said.

And so they were brought out.   Ellen
received them with stolid indifference;
Jane with indignation, if the slamming
of doors in various parts of the house that
day betokened anything.   Norah accepted them without a murmur.   It made no

difference to Norah on what day she swept the parlor, nor did she seem to care very much because her "days at home" were shifted, so that her day out was Friday instead of Thursday.

"Has Ellen said anything about the rules, my dear?" asked Thaddeus, a week or two later.

"Not a word," returned Bessie.

"Has she 'looked' anything?"

"Volumes," Bessie answered.

"Does she take exception to any of them?"

"No," said Bessie, "and I've discovered why, too. She hasn't read them."

Thaddeus was silent for a minute. Then he said, quite firmly for him, "She must read them."

"*Must* is a strong word, Teddy," Bessie replied, "particularly since Ellen can't read."

"Then you ought to read them to her."

"That's what I think," Bessie answered, amiably. "I'm going to do it very soon—day after to-morrow, I guess."

"What has Jane said?" asked Thaddeus, biting his lip.

Bessie colored. Jane had expressed herself with considerable force, and Bessie had been a little afraid to tell Thaddeus what she had said and done.

"Oh, nothing much," she answered. "She—she said she'd never worn caps like a common servant, and wasn't going to begin now; and then she didn't like having to clean the silver on Saturday afternoons, because the silver-powder got into her finger-nails; and that really is too bad, Teddy, because Saturday night is the night her friends come to call, and silver-powder is awfully hard to get out of your nails, you know; and, of course, a girl wants to appear neat and clean when she has callers."

"Of course," said Thaddeus. "And I judge by the appearance of the brass fenders that she doesn't like to polish them up on Wednesday because it gives her a backache on Thursday, which is her day out."

Bessie's eyes took on their watery aspect again.

"Do the fenders look so very badly, Ted?" she asked.

"They're atrocious," said Thaddeus.

"I'm sorry, dear; but I did my best. I polished them myself this afternoon; Jane had to go to a funeral."

"Oh, my!" cried Thaddeus. "This subject's too much for me. Let's go out — somewhere, anywhere—to a concert. Music hath its charms to soothe a savage breast, and my breast is simply the very essence of wildness to - night. Put on your things, Bess, and hurry, or I'll suffocate."

Bessie did as she was told, and before ten o'clock the happy pair had forgotten their woes, nor do I think they would have remembered them again that night had they not found on their return home that they were locked out.

At this even the too amiable Bessie was angry—very angry—unjustly, as it turned out afterwards.

"They weren't to blame, after all,"
she explained to Thaddeus, when he came
home the next night. "I spoke to them
about it, and they all thought we'd spend
the night with your mother and father
at the Oxford."

"They're a thoughtful lot," said Thaddeus.

And so time passed. The "treasures"
did as they pleased ; the dubious auburn-
haired Norah continued her aggravating
efficiency. Bessie's days were spent in an-
ticipation of an interview of an unpleasant nature with Jane or Ellen "to-morrow." Thaddeus's former smile grew less
perpetual — that is, it was always visible when Bessie was before him, but
when Bessie was elsewhere, so also was
the token of Thaddeus's amiability. He
chafed under the tyranny, but it never
occurred to him but once that it would
be well for him to interview Ellen and
Jane ; and then, summoning them fierce-
ly, he addressed them mildly, ended the
audience with a smile, and felt him-

self beneath their sway more than
ever.

Then something happened. A day
came and went, and the morrow thereof
found Thaddeus dethroned from even his
nominal position of head of the house.
There was a young Thaddeus, an eight-
pound Thaddeus, a round, red-cheeked,
bald-headed Thaddeus that looked more
like the Thaddeus of old than Thaddeus
did himself ; and then, at a period in
which man feels himself the least among
the insignificant, did our hero find happi-
ness unalloyed once more, for to the pride
of being a father was added the satisfaction of seeing Jane and Ellen acknowl-
edge a superior. Make no mistake, you
who read. It was not to Thaddeus junior
that these gems bowed down. It was to
the good woman who came in to care for
the little one and his mother that they
humbled themselves.

"She's great," said Thaddeus to himself, as he watched Jane bustling about
to obey the command of the temporary

mistress of the situation as she had never
bustled before.

"She's a second Elizabeth," chuckled
Thaddeus, as he listened to an order
passed down the dumb-waiter shaft from
the stout empress of the moment to the
trembling queen of the kitchen.

"She's a little dictatorial," whispered
Thaddeus to his newspaper, when the
monarch of all she surveyed gave him *his*
orders. "But there are times, even in a
Republic like this, when a dictator is an
advantage. I hate to see a woman cry,
but the way Jane wept at the routing Mrs.
Brown gave her this morning was a finer
sight than Niagara."

But, alas! this happy state of affairs
could not last forever. Thaddeus was
just beginning to get on easy terms with
Mrs. Brown when she was summoned
elsewhere.

"Change of heir is necessary for one
in her profession," sighed Thaddeus; and
then, when he thought of resuming the
reins himself, he sighed again, and wished

that Mrs. Brown might have remained a fixture in the household forever. "Still," he added, more to comfort himself than because he had any decided convictions to express—"still, a baby in the house will make a difference, and Ellen and Jane will behave better now that Bessie's added responsibilities put them more upon their honor."

For a time Thaddeus's prophecy was correct. Ellen and Jane did do better for nearly two months, and then—but why repeat the old story ? Then they lapsed, that is all, and became more tyrannical than ever. Bessie was so busy with little Ted that the household affairs outside of the nursery came under their exclusive control. Thaddeus stood it—I was going to say nobly, but I think it were better put ignobly— but he had a good excuse for so doing.

"A baby is an awful care to its mother," he said; "a responsibility that takes up her whole time and attention. I don't think I'd better complicate matters by getting into a row with the servants."

And so it went. A year and another
year passed. The pretty home was beginning to look old. The bloom of its youth
had most improperly faded—for surely a
home should never fade—but there was
the boy, a growing delight to his father,
so why complain ? Better this easy-going
life than one of domestic contention.

Then on a sudden the boy fell ill. The
doctor came—shook his head gravely.

" You must take him to the sea-shore,"
he said. " It is his only chance."

And to the sea-shore they went, leaving
the house in charge of the treasures.

" I have confidence in you," said Thaddeus to Jane and Ellen on the morning of
the departure, " so I have decided to leave
the house open in your care. Mrs. Perkins
wants you to keep it as you would if she
were here. Whatever you need to make
yourselves comfortable, you may get.
Good-bye."

" What a comfort it is," said Bessie,
when they had reached the sea-shore, and
were indulging in their first bit of that

woful luxury, homesickness — "what a comfort it is to feel that the girls are there to look after things! An empty house is such a temptation to thieves."

"Yes," said Thaddeus. "I hope they won't entertain too much, though."

"Ellen and Jane are too old for that sort of thing," Bessie answered.

"How about Norah?"

"Oh, I forgot to tell you. There was nothing really for Norah to do, so I told her she could go off and stay with her mother on board-wages."

"Good!" said Thaddeus, with a pleased smile. "It isn't a bad idea to save, particularly when you are staying at the sea-shore."

In this contented frame of mind they lived for several weeks. The boy grew stronger every day, and finally Thaddeus felt that the child was well enough to warrant his running back home for a night, "just to see how things were going." That the girls were faithful, of course, he did not doubt; the regularity

with which letters addressed to him at
home—and they were numerous—reached
him convinced him of that; but the hamper containing the week's wash, which
Ellen and Jane were to send, and which
had been expected on Thursday of the
preceding week, had failed for once to arrive; the boy had worn one dress four
days, Thaddeus's collars were getting low,
and altogether he was just a little uneasy
about things. So he availed himself of his
opportunity and went home, taking with
him a friend, in consideration of whom he
telegraphed ahead to Ellen to prepare a
good breakfast, not caring for dinner,
since he and his companion expected to
dine at the club and go to the theatre before going out to his home.

The result would have been fatal to
Bessie's peace of mind had she heard of
it during her absence from home. But
Thaddeus never told her, until it was a
matter of ancient history, that when he
arrived at home, a little after midnight,
he found the place deserted, and was com-

pelled to usher his friend in through the
parlor window; that from top to bottom
the mansion gave evidence of not having
seen a broom or a dust-brush since the
departure of the family; that Jane had
not been seen in the neighborhood for one
full week—this came from those living on
adjoining property; that Ellen had been
absent since early that morning, and was
not expected to return for three days;
and, crowning act of infamy, that he,
Thaddeus, and his friend were compelled
to breakfast next morning upon a half of
a custard pie, a bit mouldy, found by the
lord of the manor on the fast-melting remains of a cake of ice in the refrigerator.
Whether it would have happened if Thaddeus had not been accompanied by a
friend, whose laughter incited him to
great deeds, or not I am not prepared to
say, but something important did happen.   Thaddeus rose to the occasion, and
committed an act, and committed it thoroughly.   The Thaddeus of old, the meek,
long-suffering, too amiable Thaddeus, dis-

appeared. The famous smile was given no
chance to play. His wife was absent, and
the smile was far away with her. Thaddeus, with one fell blow, burst his fetters
and became free.

That afternoon, when he had returned
to the seaboard, Bessie asked him, "How
was the house?"

"Beautiful," said Thaddeus, quite
truthfully; for it was.

"Did Ellen say anything about the
hamper?"

"Not a word."

"Did you speak to her about it?"

"Nope."

"Oh, Teddy! How could you forget
it?"

To the lasting honor of Thaddeus be
it said that he bore up under this un-
flinchingly.

"Did you have a good breakfast, Ted?"
Bessie asked, returning to the subject
later.

"Very," said Thaddeus, thinking of the
hearty meal he and his fellow - sufferer

had eaten at the club after getting back
to town. "We had a tomato omelet, coffee, toast, rice cakes, tenderloin steak, and
grits."

"Dear me !" smiled Bessie ; she was so
glad her Teddy had been so well treated.
"All that ? Ellen must have laid herself out."

"Yes," said Thaddeus ; "I think she
did."

All the following week Thaddeus seemed to have a load on his mind—a load
which he resolutely refused to share with
his wife—and on Friday he found it necessary to go up to town.

"I thought this was your vacation,"
remonstrated Bessie.

"Well, so it is," said Thaddeus. "But
—but I've got one or two matters to attend to — matters of very great impor-
tance — so that I think I'll have to
go."

"If you must, you must," said Bessie.
"But I think it's horrid of your partner

to make you go back to town this hot
weather."

" Don't be cross with my partner," said
Thaddeus; "especially my partner in this
matter."

" Have you different partners for different matters ?" queried Bessie.

" Never mind about that, my dear ;
you'll know all about it in time, so don't
worry."

" All right, Teddy.   But I don't like
to have you running away from me when
I'm at a hotel.   I'd rather be home, anyhow.   Can't I go with you ?   Little Ted
is well enough now to go home."

" Not this time ; but you can go up
next Wednesday if you wish," returned
Thaddeus, with a slight show of embar-
rassment.

And so it was settled, and Thaddeus
went to town.   On Wednesday they all
left the sea-shore to return to Phillipse-
burg.

" Oh, how lovely it looks !" ejaculated
Bessie, as she entered the house, Norah

having opened the door. "But — er — where's Jane, Norah ?"

"Cookin' the dinner, mim."

"Why, Jane can't cook."

"If you please, mim, this is a new Jane."

Bessie's parasol fell to the floor. "A wha-a-at ?" she cried.

"A new Jane. Misther Perkins has dispinsed with old Jane and Ellen, mim."

Bessie rushed up-stairs to her room and cried. The shock was too sudden. She longed for Thaddeus, who had remained at the station collecting the bath-tubs and other luxuries of the baby from the luggage-van, to come. What did it all mean ? Jane and Ellen gone ! New girls in their places !

And then Thaddeus came, and made all plain to the little woman, and when he was all through she was satisfied. He had discharged the tyrants, and had supplied their places. The latter was the important business which had taken him to town.

"But, Teddy," Bessie said, with a smile, when she had heard all, "how did

poor mild little you ever have the courage
to face those two women and give them
their discharge ?"

Teddy blushed. "I didn't," he answered, meekly ; "I wrote it."

Five years have passed since then, and
all has gone well. Thaddeus has remained
free, and, as he proudly observes, domestics now tremble at his approach—that is,
all except Norah, who remembers him as
of old. Ellen and Jane are living together in affluence, having saved their wages
for 'nearly the whole of their term of
"service." Bessie is happy in the possession of two fine boys, to whom all her attention — all save a little reserved for
Thaddeus—is given; and, as for the dubious, auburn-haired, and distinctly Celtic
Norah, Thaddeus is afraid that she is developing into a "treasure."

"Why do you think so ?" Bessie asked
him, when he first expressed that fear.

"Oh, she has the symptoms," returned
Thaddeus. "She has taken three nights
off this week."

MR. BRADLEY'S JEWEL

MR. BRADLEY'S JEWEL

THADDEUS was tired, and, therefore, Thaddeus was grumpy. One premise only was necessary for the conclusion—in fact, it was the only premise upon which a conclusion involving Thaddeus's grumpiness could find a foothold. If Thaddeus felt rested, everything in the world could go wrong and he would smile as sweetly as ever ; but with the slightest trace of weariness in his system the smile would fade, wrinkles would gather on his forehead, and grumpiness set in whether things were right or wrong. On this special occasion to which I refer, things were just wrong enough to give him a decent excuse—outside of his weariness—for his irritation. Norah, the housemaid, had officiously undertaken to cover up the shortcomings of John, who should have blacked Thaddeus's boots, and who had taken his day off without preparing the extra pair which the lord of the manor had expected to wear that evening. It was nice of the housemaid, of course, to try to black the extra pair to keep John out of trouble, but she might have been more discriminating. It was not necessary for her to polish, until they shone like Claude Lorraine glasses, two right boots, one of which, paradoxical as it may seem, was consequently the wrong boot; so that when Thaddeus came to dress for the evening's diversion there was nowhere to be found in his shoe-box a bit of leathern gear in which his left foot might appear in polite society to advantage. Possibly Thaddeus might have endured the pain of a right boot on a left foot, had not Norah unfortunately chosen for that member a box-toed boot, while for the right she had selected one with a very decided acute angle at its toe-end.

"Just like a woman!" ejaculated Thaddeus, angrily.

"Yes," returned Bessie, missing Thaddeus's point slightly. "It was very thoughtful of Norah to look after John's work, knowing how important it was to you."

Fortunately Thaddeus was out of breath trying to shine up the other pointed-toe shoe, so that his only reply to this was a look, which Bessie, absorbed as she was in putting the studs in Thaddeus's shirt, did not see. If she had seen it, I doubt if she would have been so entirely happy as the tender little song she was humming softly to herself seemed to indicate that she was.

"Some people are born lucky!" growled Thaddeus, as he finished rubbing up the left boot, giving it a satin finish which hardly matched the luminous brilliance of its mate, though he said it would do. "There's Bradley, now; he never has any domestic woes of this sort, and he pays just half what we do for his servants."

"Oh, Mr. Bradley. I don't like him!" ejaculated Bessie. "You are always talking about Mr. Bradley, as if he had an automaton for a servant."

"No, I don't say he has an automaton," returned Thaddeus. "Automatons don't often work, and Bradley's jewel does. Her name is Mary, but Bradley always calls her his jewel."

"I've heard of jewels," said Bessie, thinking of the two Thaddeus and she had begun their married life with, "but they've always seemed to me to be paste emeralds—awfully green, and not worth much."

"There's no paste emerald about Bradley's girl," said Thaddeus. "Why, he says that woman has been in Mrs. Bradley's employ for seven weeks now, and she hasn't broken a bit of china; never sweeps dust under the beds or bureaus; keeps the silver polished so that it looks as if it were solid; gets up at six every morning; cooks well; is civil, sober, industrious; has no hangers-on—"

"Is Mr. Bradley a realist or a romancer?" asked Bessie.

"Why do you ask that?" replied Thaddeus.

"That jewel story sounds like an *Arabian Nights* tale," said Bessie. "I don't believe that it is more than half true, and that half is exaggerated."

"Well, it *is* true," said Thaddeus. "And, what is more, the girl helps in the washing, plays with the children, and on her days out she stays at home and does sewing."

Bessie laughed. "She must be a regular Koh-i-noor," she said. "I suppose Mr. Bradley pays her a thousand dollars a month."

"No, he doesn't; he pays her twelve," said Thaddeus.

"Then he is just what I said he was," snapped Bessie—"a mean thing. The idea —twelve dollars a month for all that! Why, if she could prove she was all that you say she is, she could make ten times that amount by exhibiting herself. She is

a curiosity. But if I were Mrs. Bradley I
wouldn't have her in the house. So many
virtues piled one on the other are sure to
make an unsafe structure, and I believe
some poor, miserable little vice will crop
out somewhere and upset the whole thing."

"You are jealous," said Thaddeus; and
then he went out.

The next day, meeting his friend Bradley on the street, Thaddeus greeted him
with a smile, and said, "Mrs. Perkins
thinks you ought to take up literature."

"Why so?" asked Bradley.

"She thinks De Foe and Scott and
Dumas and Stevenson would be thrown
into the depths of oblivion if you were to
write up that jewel of yours," said Thaddeus. "She thinks your Mary is one of
the finest, most imaginative creations of
modern days."

"She doubts her existence, eh?"
smiled Bradley.

"Well, she thinks she's more likely to
be a myth than a Smith," said Thaddeus.
"She told me to ask you if Mary has a

twin-sister, and to say that if you hear of
her having any relatives at all—and no
domestic ever lived who hadn't—to send
her their addresses. She'd like to employ
a few."

"I am sorry Mrs. Perkins is so blinded
by jealousy," said Bradley, with a smile.
"And I regret to say that Mary hasn't a
cousin on the whole police force, or, in
fact, any kind of a relative whatsoever,
unless she prevaricates."

"Too bad," said Thaddeus. "I had a
vague hope we could stock up on jewels
of her kind. Where did you get her, anyhow—Tiffany's?"

"No. At an unintelligence office,"
said Bradley. "She was a last resort.
We had to have some one, and she was the
only girl there. We took her for a week
on trial without references, and, by Jove!
she turned out a wonder."

Thaddeus grinned, and said: "Give
her time, Bradley. By-the-way, at what
hours is she on exhibition? I'd like to
see her."

"Come up to-night and test the truth of what I say," said Bradley. "I won't let anybody know you are coming, and you'll see her just as we see her. What do you say?"

The temptation was too strong for Thaddeus to resist, and so it was that Bessie received a telegram that afternoon from her beloved, stating that he would dine with Bradley, and return home on a late train. The telegram concluded with the line, *"I'm going to appraise the escaped crown-jewel."*

Bessie chuckled at this, and stayed up until long after the arrival of the last train, so interested was she to hear from Thaddeus all about the Bradley jewel, who, as she said, "seemed too good to be true"; but she was finally forced to retire disappointed and somewhat anxious, for Thaddeus did not return home that night.

Somewhere in the neighborhood of eight o'clock the next morning Bessie received a second telegram, which read as follows :

*"Do not worry. I am all right. Will
be home about nine. Have breakfast."*

"Now I wonder what on earth can have
kep thim?" Bessie said. "Something has
happened, I am sure. Perhaps an accident
on the elevated, or maybe—"

She did not finish the sentence, but
rushed into the library and snatched up
the morning paper, scanning its every
column in the expectation, if not hope,
of finding that some horrible disaster had
occurred, in which her Thaddeus might
have been involved. The paper disclosed
nothing of the sort. Only a few common-
place murders, the usual assortment of
defalcations, baseball prophecies, and po-
litical prognostications could Bessie discover therein. Never, in fact, had the
newspaper seemed so uninteresting—not
even a bargain-counter announcement was
there—and with an impatient, petulant
stamp of her little foot she threw the jour-
nal from her and returned to the dining-
room. It was then half-past eight, and,
hardly able to contain herself with excite-

ment, Bessie sat down by the window,
and almost, if not quite, counted every
swing of the pendulum that pushed the
hands of the clock on to the desired hour.
She could not eat, and not until her curiosity was gratified as to what it was that
had detained Thaddeus, and that, more
singular still, was bringing him home instead of sending him to business at nine
o'clock in the morning, could she, in fact,
do anything ?

Finally, the grinding sounds of carriage
wheels on the gravel road without were
heard, and in an instant Bessie was at the
door to welcome the prodigal. And what
a Thaddeus it was that came home that
morning ! His eyes showed conclusively
that he had had no sleep, save the more
or less unsatisfactory napping which suburban residents get on the trains. His
beautiful pearl-gray scarf, that so became
him when he left home the previous morning, was not anywhere in sight. His
cheek was scratched, and every button
that his vest had ever known had taken

wings unto itself and flown, Bessie knew
not whither. And yet, tired out as he
was, dishevelled as he was, Thaddeus was
not grumpy, but inclined rather to explo-
sive laughter as he entered the house.

"Why, Thaddeus!" cried Bessie, in
alarm. "What on earth is the matter with
you? You look as if you had been in a
riot."

"That's a pretty good guess, my dear,"
returned Thaddeus, with a laugh, "but
not quite the right one."

"But tell me, what have you been doing? Where have you been?"

"At Bradley's, my love."

"You haven't been—been quarrelling
with Mr. Bradley?"

"No. Bradley's jewel has proved your
husband's Waterloo, as well as the Sedan
of Bradley himself," returned Thaddeus,
throwing his head back and bursting out
into a loud guffaw.

"I am not good at riddles, Thaddeus,"
said Bessie, "and I haven't laughed much
myself since that last train came in last

night and didn't bring you. I think you might tell me—"

"Why, my dear little girl," said Thaddeus, walking to her side and kissing her, "I didn't mean to keep you in suspense, and of course I'll tell you."

Then, as they ate their breakfast, Thaddeus explained. "I told Bradley that you were a sceptic on the subject of his jewel," he said, "and he offered to prove that she was eighteen carats fine by taking me home with him, an unexpected guest, by which act he would test her value to my satisfaction. Of course, having cast doubts upon her excellence, I had to accept, and at half-past five he and I boarded an elevated train for Harlem. At six we stood before Bradley's front door, and as he had left his keys at the office, he rang the bell and waited. It was a long wait, considering the presence of a jewel within doors. It must have lasted fifteen minutes, and even that would have been but the beginning, in spite of repeated and continuous pulling of the bell-handle, had we not determined to enter through the reception-room window."

"Did you try the basement door?" queried Bessie, with a smile, for it pleased her to hear that the jewel was not quite flawless.

"Yes," said Thaddeus. "We rang four times at the basement, and I should say seven times at the front door, and then we took to the window. Bradley's is one of those narrow English-basement houses with a small yard in front, so that the reception-room window is easy to reach by climbing over the vault leading to the basement door, which is more or less of a cellar entrance. Fortunately the window was unlocked. I say fortunately, because it enabled us to get into the house, though if I were sitting on a jury I think I should base an indictment — one of criminal negligence—of the jewel on the fact that it was unlocked. It was just the hour, you know, when policemen yawn and sneak-thieves prowl."

"How careless!" vouchsafed Bessie.

"Very," said Thaddeus. "But this time it worked for the good of all concerned, although my personal appearance doesn't give any indication that I gained anything by it. In fact, it would have been better for me if the house had been hermetically sealed."

"Don't dally so much, Thaddeus," put in Bessie. "I'm anxious to hear what happened."

"Well, of course Bradley was very much concerned," continued Thaddeus. "It was bad enough not to be able to attract the maid's attention by ringing, but when he noticed that the house was as dark as pitch, and that despite the clanging of the bell, which could be heard all over the neighborhood, even his wife didn't come to the door, he was worried; and he was more worried than ever when he got inside. We lit the gas in the hall, and walked back into the dining-room, where we also lighted up, and such confusion as was there you never saw! The table-cloth was in a heap on the

floor; Bradley's candelabra, of which he
was always so proud, were bent and twist-
ed out of shape under the table; glasses
broken beyond redemption were strewn
round about; and a mixture of pepper,
salt, and sugar was over everything."

"'I believe there have been thieves
here,' said Bradley, his face turning
white.   And then he went to the foot of
the stairs and called up to his wife, but
there was no answer.

"Then he started on a dead run up
the stair.   Above all was in confusion, as
in the dining-room.   Vases were broken,
pictures hung awry on the walls; but
nowhere was Mrs. Bradley or one of the
Bradley children to be seen.

"Then we began a systematic search of
the house.   Everywhere everything was
upsidedown, and finally we came to a
door on the third story back, leading
into the children's play-room, and as
we turned the knob and tried to open
it we heard Mrs. Bradley's voice from
within.

" ' Who's there ?' she said, her voice all of a tremble.

" ' It is I !' returned Bradley. 'Open the door. What is the meaning of all this ?'

" ' Oh, I'm so glad you have come !' returned Mrs. Bradley, with a sob, and then we heard sounds as of the moving of heavy furniture. Mrs. Bradley, for some as yet unexplained reason, seemed to have. barricaded herself in.

" Finally the door was opened, and Mrs. Bradley buried her face on her husband's shoulder and sobbed hysterically.

" ' What on earth is the matter ?' asked Bradley, as his children followed their mother's lead, except that they buried their faces in his coat-tail pockets. ' What has happened ?'

" ' Mary !' gasped Mrs. Bradley."

" The jewel ?" asked Bessie.

" The same," returned Thaddeus, with a smile. " She was the jewel, alas ! now deprived of her former glorious setting.

" ' What's the matter with Mary ?' asked Bradley.

"'She's been behaving outrageously. I found her this morning,' said Mrs. Bradley, 'rummaging through my escritoire, throwing things all over the floor; and when I remonstrated she said she was looking for a sheet of paper on which to write a letter. I told her she should have asked me for it, and she replied impertinently that she never asked favors of anybody. I told her to leave the room, and she declined to do it, picking up a sofa-pillow and throwing it at me. I was so overcome I nearly fainted.'"

"I should think she would have been overcome! Such impudence!" said Bessie.

"Humph!" said Thaddeus. "That isn't a marker to what followed. Why, according to Mrs. Bradley's story, that escaped Koh-i-noor called her all sorts of horrible names, threw an empty ink-pot at a photograph of Bradley himself, that stood on the mantel, and then, grabbing up a whisk-broom, literally swept everything else there was on the mantel off to the

floor with it. This done, she began to
overturn chairs with an ardor born of
temper, apparently; and, finally, Mrs.
Bradley got so frightened that she ran
from the room, and the jewel started in
pursuit. Straight to the nursery ran the
lady of the house—for there was where
the children were, playing house, no
doubt, with little idea that jewels sometimes deteriorated. Once in the nursery,
Mrs. Bradley slammed the door to, locked
it, and then, still fearful, rolled before it
the bureau and the children's cribs. After that the actions of the jewel could only
be surmised. The door was pounded and
the atmosphere of the hall was rent with
violent harangues; then a hurried step
was heard as the jewel presumably sailed
below-stairs; then crashings were heard—
crashings which might have indicated the
smashing of windows, of picture-glass, of
mirrors, chairs, and other household ap-
purtenances, after which, Mrs. Bradley observed, all became still."

"Mercy! what a trial!" said Bessie.

"And was she locked up in the nursery all day ?"

"From twelve until we rescued her at a little after six," said Thaddeus. "Then Bradley and I started out to find the jewel, if possible, and I regret to say that it was possible. We found her asleep on the kitchen table, and Bradley hadn't any more sense than to try and wake her up. He succeeded too well. For the next ten minutes she was the most wide-awake woman you ever saw, and she kept us wide awake too. The minute she opened her eyes and saw us standing before her, she sprang to her feet and made a rush at Bradley, for which he was totally unprepared, the consequence of which was that in an instant he found himself sitting in a very undignified manner, for the head of the house, on the kitchen floor, trying to collect his somewhat scattered faculties.

"When she had persuaded Bradley to take a seat, she turned to shower her attentions on me. I jumped to one side,

but she managed to grab hold of my vest,
and hence its buttonless condition. By
this time Bradley was on his feet again,
and, having had the temerity to face his
jewel the second time, he again came off
second best, losing one of the button-
holes of his collar in the mêlée. I rushed
in from behind, and flirtatiously, perhaps, tried to grab hold of her hands,
coming off the field minus a necktie, but
plus that picturesque scratch you see on
my nose. Stopping a moment to count
up my profit and loss, I let Bradley make
the next assault, which resulted in a
drawn battle, Bradley losing his watch
and his temper, the jewel losing her
breath and her balance. So it went on
for probably three or four minutes longer,
though we certainly acquired several years
of experience in those short minutes,
until finally we managed to conquer her.
This done, we locked her up in a closet."

"Had she been at the cooking-sherry?"
asked Bessie.

"We thought so at first, and Bradley

sent for a policeman," said Thaddeus;
"but when he came we found the poor
creature too exhausted to be moved, and in
a very short while Mrs. Bradley decided
that it was a case for a doctor and not
for a police-justice. So the doctor was
summoned, and we waited, dinnerless, in
the dining-room for his verdict, and
finally it came. *Bradley's jewel was insane!*"

"Insane!" echoed Bessie.

"Mad as a hatter," replied Thaddeus.

"Well, I declare!" said Bessie, thought-
fully. "But, Thaddeus, do you know I
am not surprised."

"Why, my dear?" he asked.

"Because, Teddy, she was too perfect
to be in her right mind."

And Thaddeus, after thinking it all
over, was inclined to believe that Bessie
was in the right.

"Yes, Bess, she was perfect—perfect
in the way she did her work, perfect in the
way she smashed things, and nowhere did
she more successfully show the thorough-

ness with which she did everything than
when it came to removing the buttons
from my vest. Isn't it too bad that
the only perfect servant that ever lived
should turn out to be a hopeless maniac?
But I must hurry off, or I'll miss my
train."

"You are not going down to town to-
day?" asked Bessie.

"To-day, above all other days, am I
going down," returned Thaddeus. "I
am enough of a barbarian to be unwilling
to lose the chance of seeing Bradley, and
asking him how he and his jewel get
along."

"Thaddeus!"

"Why not, my dear?"

"It would be too mean for anything."

"Well, perhaps you are right. I guess
I won't. But he has rubbed it into me
so much about our domestics that I hate
to lose the chance to hit back."

"Has he?" said Bessie, her face flush-
ing indignantly, and, it may be added,
becomingly. "In that case, perhaps,

you might—ha! ha!—perhaps you might telegraph and ask him."

And Thaddeus did so. As yet he has received no reply.

UNEXPECTED POMP AT THE PERKINS'S

UNEXPECTED POMP AT THE
PERKINS'S

"My dear," said Thaddeus, one night,
as he and Mrs. Perkins entered the library
after dinner, "that was a very good dinner to-night. Don't you think so?"

"All except the salmon," said Bessie,
with a smile.

"Salmon?" echoed Thaddeus. "Salmon? I did not see any salmon."

"No," said Bessie, "that was just the
trouble. It didn't come up, although it
was in the house before dinner, I'm certain. I saw it arrive."

"Ellen couldn't have known you in-
tended it for dinner," said Thaddeus.

"Yes, she knew it was for dinner," returned Bessie, "but she made a mistake
as to whose dinner it was for. She sup-

posed it was bought for the kitchen-table, and when I went down-stairs to inquire about it a few minutes ago it was fulfilling its assumed mission nobly. There wasn't much left but the tail and one fin."

" Well !" ejaculated Thaddeus, " I call that a pretty cool proceeding. Did you give her a talking to ?"

" No," Bessie replied, shortly ; " I despise a domestic fuss, so I pretended I'd gone down to talk about breakfast. We'll have breakfast an hour or two earlier to-morrow, dear."

" What's that for ?" queried Thaddeus, his eyes open wide with astonishment. " You are not going shopping, are you ?"

" No, Teddy, I'm not ; but when I got down-stairs and realized that Ellen had made the natural mistake of supposing the fish was for the down-stairs dinner, this being Friday, I had to think of something to say, and nothing would come except that we wanted breakfast at seven instead of at eight. It doesn't do to have servants suspect you of spying upon them,

nor is it wise ever to appear flustered—so
mamma says—in their presence. I avoid-
ed both by making Ellen believe I'd come
down to order an early breakfast."

"You are a great Bessie," said Thaddeus, with a laugh. "I admire you more
than ever, my dear, and to prove it I'd get
up to breakfast if you'd ordered it at 1 A.M."

"You'd be more likely to stay up to it,"
said Bessie, "and then go to bed after it."

"There's your Napoleonic mind again,"
said Thaddeus. "I should never have
thought of that way out of it. But, Bess,"
he continued, "when I was praising to-
night's dinner I had a special object in
view. I think Ellen cooks well enough
now to warrant us in giving a dinner,
don't you?"

"Well, it all depends on what we have
for dinner," said Bessie. "Ellen's bis-
cuits are atrocious, I think, and you know
how lumpy the oatmeal always is."

"Suppose we try giving a dinner with
the oatmeal and biscuit courses left out?"
suggested Thaddeus, with a grin.

Bessie's eyes twinkled. "You make very bright after-dinner speeches, Teddy," she said. "I don't see why we can't have a dinner with nothing but pretty china, your sparkling conversation, and a few flowers strewn about. It would be particularly satisfactory to me."

"They're not all angels like you, my dear," Thaddeus returned. "There's Bradley, for instance. He'd die of starvation before we got to the second course in a dinner of that kind, and if there is any one thing that can cast a gloom over a dinner, it is to have one of the guests die of starvation right in the middle of it."

"Mr. Bradley would never do so ungentlemanly a thing," said Bessie, laughing heartily. "He is too considerate a man for that; he'd starve in silence and without ostentation."

"Why this sudden access of confidence in Bradley?" queried Thaddeus. "I thought you didn't like him?"

"Neither I did, until that Sunday he

spent with us," Bessie answered. "I've admired him intensely ever since. Don't you remember, we had lemon pie for dinner—one I made myself?"

"Yes, I remember," said Thaddeus; "but I fail to see the connection between lemon pie and Bradley. Bradley is not sour or crusty."

"You wouldn't have failed to see if you'd watched Mr. Bradley at dinner," retorted Bessie. "He ate two pieces of it."

"And just because a man eats two pieces of lemon pie prepared by your own fair hands you whirl about, and, from utterly disliking him, call him, upon the whole, one of the most admirable products of the human race?" said Thaddeus.

"Not at all," Bessie replied, with a broad smile; "but I did admire the spirit and politeness of the man. On our way home from church in the morning we were talking about the good times children have on their little picnics, and Mr. Bradley said he never enjoyed a pic-

nic in his life, because every one he had
ever gone to was ruined by the baleful
influence of lemon pie."

Thaddeus laughed. " Then he didn't
like lemon pie ?" he asked.

" No, he hated it," said Bessie, joining
in the laugh. " He added that the original receipt for it came out of Pandora's
box."

" Poor   Bradley !" cried Thaddeus,
throwing his head back in a paroxysm
of mirth. "Hated pie—declared his feelings—and then to be confronted by it at
dinner."

" He behaved nobly," said Bessie. " Ate
his first piece like a man, and then called
for a second, like a hero, when you remarked that it was of my make."

" You ought to have told him it wasn't
necessary, Bess," said Thaddeus.

" I felt that way myself at first," Bessie explained ; " but then I thought I
wouldn't let him know I remembered
what he had said."

"I fancy that was better," said Thaddeus. "But about that dinner. What do you say to our inviting the Bradleys, Mr. and Mrs. Phillips, the Robinsons, and the Twinings?"

"How many does that make? Eight besides ourselves?" asked Bessie, counting upon her fingers.

"Yes—ten altogether," said Thaddeus.

"It can't be done, dear," said Bessie. "We have only eight fruit plates."

"Can't you and I go without fruit?" Thaddeus asked.

"Not very well," laughed Bessie. "It would never do."

"They might think the fruit was poisoned if we did, eh?" suggested Thaddeus.

"Besides, Mary never could serve dinner for ten; eight is her number. Last time we had ten people, don't you remember, she dropped a tray full of dishes, and poured the claret into the champagne glasses?"

"Oh, yes, so she did," said Thaddeus. "That's how we came to have only eight

fruit plates. I remember. I don't think
it was the number of people at the table, though. It was Twining caused the
trouble. He had just made the pleasant
remark that he wouldn't have an Irish
servant in his house, when Mary fired the
salute."

"Then that settles it," said Bessie.
"We'll cut the Twinings out, and ask the
others. I don't care much for Mrs.
Twining, anyhow; she's nothing but
clothes and fidgets."

"And Twining doesn't do much but ask
you what you think of certain things, and
then tell you you are all wrong when he
finds out," said Thaddeus. "Yes, it's
just as well to cut them off this time.
We'll make it for eight, and have it a
week from Thursday night."

"That's Mary's night off," said Bessie.

"Then how about having it Friday?"

"That's Maggie's night off, and there
won't be anybody to mind the baby."

"Humph!" said Thaddeus. "I wish
there were a baby safe-deposit company

somewhere. Can't your mother come over
and look after him ?"

" No," said Bessie, " she can't. The
child always develops something every
time mother comes. Not, of course, that
I believe she gives it to him, but she looks
for things, don't you know."

" Yes," said Thaddeus, " I know. Then
make it Wednesday. That's my busy day
down-town, and I sha'n't be able to get
home much before half-past six, but if dinner is at seven, there will be time enough
for me to dress."

" Very well," said Bessie. " I will write
the invitations to-morrow, and, meanwhile,
you and I can get up the menu."

" Oysters to begin with, of course," said
Thaddeus.

" I suppose so," said Bessie, " though,
you remember, the last time we had oysters you had to open them, because the
man from the market didn't get here until half-past seven."

" And Ellen had never opened any except with a tack-hammer," said Thaddeus.

"Yes, I remember. But lightning never strikes twice in the same place. Put down the oÿsters. Then we'll have some kind of a purée—celery purée, eh ?"

"That will be very good if Ellen can be induced to keep it thick."

"Perhaps we'd better tell her we want a celery consommé," suggested Thaddeus. "Then it will be sure to be as thick as a dictionary."

"I guess it will be all right," said Bessie. "What kind of fish ?"

"Bradley likes salmon ; Robinson likes sole; Phillips likes whitebait, and so do I."

"We'll have whitebait," said Bessie, simply. "Then a saddle of mutton ?"

"Yes, and an entrée of some kind, and next individual ruddy ducks."

"No Roman punch ?"

"We can get along without that, I think," said Thaddeus. "We want to keep this dinner down to Mary's comprehension, and I'm afraid she wouldn't know what to make of an ice in the middle of

the dinner. The chances are she'd want
to serve it hot."

"All right, Teddy. What next?"

"I would suggest a lemon pie for Bradley," smiled Thaddeus.

"What do you say to Ellen's making
one of her tipsy-cakes?" suggested Bessie.

"Just the thing," said Thaddeus,
smacking his lips with enthusiasm. "I
could eat a million of 'em. Then we can
finish up with coffee and fruit."

So it was settled. The invitations were
sent out, and Bessie devoted her ener-
gies for the next ten days to making
ready.

Ellen's culinary powers were tested at
every meal. For dinner one night she
was requested to prepare the purée, which
turned out to be eminently satisfactory.
Thaddeus gave her a few practical lessons
in the art of opening oysters, an art of
which he had become a master in his college days—in fact, if his own words were
to be believed, it was the sole accomplish-
ment he had there acquired which gave

any significance whatever to his degree of
B. A.—so that in case the "fish gentleman" failed to appear in time nothing
disastrous might result.   Other things on
the menu were also ordered at various
times, and all went so well that when
Thaddeus left home on the chosen Wednesday morning, it was with a serene sense
of good times ahead.   The invited guests
had accepted, and everything was promising.

As Thaddeus had said, Wednesday was
his busy day, and never had it been busier
than upon this occasion.   Everything
moved smoothly, but there was a great
deal to move, and finally, when all was
done, and Thaddeus rose to leave his desk,
it was nearly six o'clock, and quite impossible for him to reach home before seven.
"I shall be late," he said, as he hurried
off; and he was right.   He arrived at
home coincidently with his guests, rushed
to his room, and dressed.   But one glimpse
had he of Bessie, and that was as they
passed on the stairs, she hurrying down

to receive her guests, he hurrying up to change his clothes.

"Oh, Thad!" was all she said, but to Thaddeus it was disconcerting.

"What is the matter, dear?" he asked.

"Nothing; I'll tell you later. Hurry," she gasped, "or the dinner will be spoiled."

Thaddeus hurried as he never hurried before, and in fifteen minutes walked, immaculate as to attire, into the drawing-room, where Bessie, her color heightened to an unusual degree, and her usually bright eyes fairly flaming with an unwonted brilliance, was entertaining the Bradleys, the Phillipses, and the Robinsons.

"Didn't expect me, did you?" said Thaddeus, as he entered the room.

"No," said Bradley, dryly. "This is an unexpected pleasure. I didn't even know you were a friend of the family."

"Well, I am," said Thaddeus. "One of the oldest friends I've got, in fact, which is my sole excuse for keeping you waiting. Old friends are privileged—eh, Mrs. Robinson?"

"Dinner is served," came a deep bass voice from the middle of the doorway.

Thaddeus jumped as if he had seen a ghost, and, turning to see what could have caused the strange metamorphosis in the soprano tremolo of Mary's voice, was astonished to observe in the parting of the portières not the more or less portly Mary, but a huge, burly, English-looking man, bowing in a most effective and graceful fashion to Mrs. Bradley, and then straightening himself up into a pose as rigid and uncompromising as that of a marble statue.

"What on earth—" began Thaddeus, with a startled look of inquiry at Bessie. But she only shook her head, and put her finger to her lips, enjoining silence, which Thaddeus, fortunately, had the good sense to understand, even if his mind was not equal to the fathoming of that other mystery, the pompous and totally unexpected butler.

But if Thaddeus was surprised to see the butler, he was amazed at the dinner which the butler served. Surely, he

thought, if Ellen can prepare a dinner
like this, she ought to be above taking
sixteen dollars and a home a month. It
was simply a regal repast. The oysters
were delicious, and the purée was superior to anything Thaddeus had ever eaten
in the line of soups in his life—only it was
lobster purée, and ten times better than
Ellen's general run of celery purée. He
winked his eye to denote his extreme satisfaction to Bessie when he thought no
one was looking, but was overwhelmed
with mortification when he observed that
the wink had been seen by the overpow-
ering butler, who looked sternly at him,
as much as to say, "'Ow wery wulgar !"

"I must congratulate your cook upon
her lobster purée, Mrs. Perkins," said Mr.
Phillips. "It is delicious."

"Yes," put in Thaddeus. "But you
ought to taste her celery purée. She is
undoubtedly great on purées."

Bessie coughed slightly and shook her
head at Thaddeus, and Thaddeus thought
he detected the germ of a smile upon the

cold face of the butler. He was not sure
about it, but it curdled his blood just a
little, because that ghost of a smile seemed to have just a tinge of a sneer in it.

"This isn't the same cook you had last
time, is it?" asked Bradley.

"Yes," said Thaddeus. "Same one,
though it was my wife who made that
lem—"

"Thaddeus," interrupted Bessie, "Mrs.
Robinson tells me that she and Mr. Robinson are going down to New York to the
theatre on Friday night. Can't we all
go?"

"Certainly," said Thaddeus. "I'm in
on any little diversion of that sort. Why,
what's this?—er—why, yes, of course.
Phillips, you'll go; and you, too, eh, Bradley?"

Thaddeus was evidently much upset
again; for, instead of the whitebait he
and Bessie had decided upon for their
fish course, the butler had entered, bearing in a toplofty fashion a huge silver
platter, upon which lay a superb salmon,

beautifully cooked and garnished. This
he was now holding before Thaddeus,
and stood awaiting his nod of approval
before serving it. Inasmuch as Thaddeus not only expected whitebait, but had
also never before seen the silver platter,
it is hardly surprising that he should sit
staring at the fish in a puzzled sort of
way. He recovered shortly, however,
gave the nod the butler was waiting for,
and the dinner proceeded. And what a
dinner it was! Each new course in
turn amazed Thaddeus far more than
the course that had preceded it; and
now, when the butler, whom Thaddeus
had got more or less used to, came in
bearing a bottle of wine, followed by
another stolid, well-dressed person, who
might have been his twin-brother and
who was in reality no more than assistant
to the other, Thaddeus began to fear that
the wine he had partaken of had brought
about that duplication of sight which is
said to be one of the symptoms of over-
indulgence. Either that or he was dream-

ing, he thought; and the alternative was
not a pleasant one, for Thaddeus did not
over-indulge, and as a person of intellect
he did not deem it the proper thing to
dream at the dinner-table, since the first
requisite of dreaming is falling asleep.
This Thaddeus never did in polite society.

To say that he could scarcely contain
himself for curiosity to know what had
occurred to bring about this singular condition of affairs is to put it with a mild-
ness which justice to Thaddeus compels
me to term criminal. Yet, to his credit
be it said, that through the whole of the
repast, which lasted for two hours, he
kept silent, and but for a slight nervous-
ness of manner no one would have sus-
pected that he was not as he had always
been. Indeed, to none of the party, not
even excepting his wife, did Thaddeus
appear to be anything but what he should
be. But when, finally, the ladies had
withdrawn and the men remained over
the coffee and cigars, he was compelled to

undergo a still severer test upon his loyalty to Bessie, whose signal to him to accept all and say nothing he was so nobly obeying.

Bradley began it. "I didn't know you'd changed from women to men servants, Perkins?"

"Yes," said Thaddeus, "we've changed. Rather good change, don't you think?"

"Splendid," said Phillips. "That fellow served the dinner like a prince."

"I don't believe he's any more than a duke, though," said Bradley. "His manner was quite ducal—in fact, too ducal, if Perkins will let me criticise. He made me feel like a poor, miserable, red-blooded son of the people. I wanted an olive, and, by Jove, I didn't dare ask for it."

"That wasn't his fault," said Robinson, with a laugh. "You forget that you live in a country where red blood is as good as blue. Where did you get him, Thaddeus?"

Thaddeus looked like a rat in a corner with a row of cats to the fore.

"Oh!—we—er—we got him from—
dear me! I never can remember. Mrs.
Perkins can tell you, though," he stam-
mered. "She looks after the menagerie."

"What's his name?" asked Phillips.

Thaddeus's mind was a blank. He
could not for the life of him think what
name a butler would be likely to have,
but in a moment he summoned up nerve
enough to speak.

"Grimmins," he said, desperately.

"Sounds like a Dickens character,"
said Robinson. "Does he cost you very
much, Thad?"

"Oh no — not so very much," said
Thaddeus, whose case was now so des-
perate that he resolved to put a stop to it
all. Unfortunately, his method of doing
so was not by telling the truth, but by a
flight of fancy in which he felt he owed
it to Bessie to indulge.

"No—he doesn't cost much," he repeated, boldly. "Fact is, he is a man
we've known for a great many years. He
—er—he used to be butler in my grand-

father's house in Philadelphia, and—er—
and I was there a great deal of the time
as a boy, and Grimmins and I were great
friends. When my grandfather died Grimmins disappeared, and until last month
I never heard a word of him, and then
he wrote to me stating that he was out
of work and poor as a fifty-cent table-
d'hôte dinner, and would like employment
at nominal wages if he could get a home
with it. We were just getting rid of our
waitress, and so I offered Grimmins thirty
a month, board, lodging, and clothes. He
came on; I gave him one of my old dress-
suits, set him to work, and there you
are."

"I thought you said a minute ago Mrs.
Perkins got him?" said Bradley, who is
one of those disagreeable men with a
memory.

"I thought you were talking about the
cook," said Thaddeus, uneasily. "Weren't
you talking about the cook?"

"No; but we ought to have been,"
said Phillips, with enthusiasm. "She's

the queen of cooks. What do you pay
her ?"

"Sixteen," said Thaddeus, glad to get
back on the solid ground of truth once
more.

"What ?" cried Phillips. "Sixteen,
and can cook like that ? Take me down
and introduce me, will you, Perkins ? I'd
like to offer her seventeen to come and
cook for me."

"Let's join the ladies," said Thaddeus,
abruptly. "There's no use of our wast-
ing our sweetness upon each other."

If the head of the house had expected
to be relieved from his unfortunate em-
barrassments by joining the ladies, he was
doomed to bitter disappointment, for the
conversation abandoned at the table was
resumed in the drawing-room. The dinner had been too much of a success to be
forgotten readily.

Thaddeus's troubles were set going again
when he overheard Phillips saying to Bessie, "Thaddeus has been telling us the
remarkable story of Grimmins."

Nor were his woes lightened any when he caught Bessie's reply: "Indeed? What story is that?"

"Why, the story of the butler—Grimmins, you know. How you came to get him, and all that," said Phillips. "Really, you are to be congratulated."

"I am glad to know you feel that way," said Bessie, simply, with a glance at Thaddeus which was full of wonderment.

"He is a treasure," said Bradley; "but your cook is a whole chestful of treasures. And how fortunate you and Thaddeus are! The idea of there being anywhere in the world a person of such ability in her vocation, and so poor a notion of her worth!"

Thaddeus breathed again, now that the cook was under discussion. He knew all about her.

"Yes, indeed," said Bessie. "He did well."

"I mean the cook," returned Bradley. "You mean she did well, don't you?"

What Bessie would have answered, or

what Thaddeus would have done next
if the conversation had been continued,
can be a matter of unprofitable specula-
tion only, for at this point a wail from
above-stairs showed that Master Perkins
had awakened, and the ladies, considerate of Bessie's maternal feelings, promptly
rose to take their leave, and in ten minutes she and Thaddeus were alone.

"What on earth is the story of Grimmins, Thaddeus?" she asked, as the door
closed upon the departing guests.

Thaddeus threw himself wearily down
upon the sofa and explained. He told
her all he had said about the butler and
the cook.

'That's the story of Grimmins," he
said, when he had finished.

"Oh, dear me, dear me!" cried Bessie,
"you told the men that, and I—I, Thaddeus, told the women the truth. Why,
it's—it's awful. You'll never hear the
end of it."

"Well, now that they know the truth,
Bess," Thaddeus said, "suppose you let

me into the secret. What on earth is the meaning of all this—two butlers, silver platters, dinner fit for the gods, and all?"

"It's all because of the tipsy-cake," said Bessie.

"The what?" asked Thaddeus, sitting up and gazing at his wife as if he questioned her sanity.

"The tipsy-cake," she repeated. "I gave Ellen the bottle of brandy you gave me for the tipsy-cake, and—and she drank half of it."

"And the other half?"

"Mary drank that. They got word this morning that their brother was very ill, and it upset them so I don't believe they knew what they were doing; but at one o'clock, when I went down to lunch, there was no lunch ready, and when I descended into the kitchen to find out why, I found that the fire had gone out, and both girls were — both girls were asleep on the cellar floor. They're there yet—locked in; and all through dinner I

was afraid they might come to, and—
make a rumpus."

"And the dinner?" said Thaddeus, a
light breaking through into his troubled
mind.

" I telegraphed to New York to Partinelli at once, telling him to serve a dinner
for eight here to-night, supplying service,
cook, dinner, and everything, and at four
o'clock these men arrived and took possession. It was the only thing I could
do, Thad, wasn't it?"

"It was, Bess," said Thaddeus, gravely.
"It was great; but—by Jove, I wish I'd
known, because— Did you really tell the
ladies the truth about it?"

"Yes, I did," said Bessie. ". They
were so full of praises for everything that
I didn't think it was fair for me to take
all the credit of it, so I told them the
whole thing."

"That was right, too," said Thaddeus;
" but those fellows will never let me hear
the end of that infernal Grimmins story.
I almost wish we—"

"You wish what, Teddy dear?"

"I almost wish we had not attempted the tipsy-cake, and had stuck to my original suggestion," said Thaddeus.

"What was that?" Bessie asked.

"To have lemon pie for dessert, for Bradley's sake," answered Thaddeus, as he locked the front door and turned off the gas.

AN OBJECT-LESSON

AN OBJECT-LESSON

IT was early in the autumn. Mr. and Mrs. Perkins, with their two hopefuls, had returned from a month of rest at the mountains, and the question of school for Thaddeus junior came up.

"He is nearly six years old," said Bessie, "and I think he is quite intelligent enough to go to school, don't you ?"

" Well, if you want my honest opinion," Thaddeus answered, "I think he's intelligent enough to go without school for another year at least. I don't want a hot-house boy, and I have always been opposed to forcing these little minds that we are called upon by circumstances to direct. It seems to me that the thing for us to do is to hold them back, if anything. If Teddy goes to school now,

he'll be ready for college when he is
twelve. He'll be graduated at sixteen,
and at twenty he'll be practising law. At
twenty-five he'll be leader of the bar ; and
then—what will there be left for him to
achieve at fifty ? Absolutely nothing."

Mrs. Perkins laughed. "You have
great hopes for Teddy, haven't you ?"

"Certainly I have," Thaddeus replied ; "and why shouldn't I ? Doesn't
he combine all my good qualities plus
yours ? How can he be anything else
than great ?"

"I am afraid there's a touch of vanity
in you," said Mrs. Perkins, with a smile.
"That remark certainly indicates it."

"No — it's not vanity in me," said
Thaddeus. "It's confidence in you.
You've assured me so often of my perfection that I am beginning to believe in
it ; and as for your perfection, I've always
believed in it. Hence, when I see Teddy
combining your perfect qualities with my
own, I regard him as a supernaturally
promising person—that is, I do until he

begins to show the influence of contact
with the hired man, and uses language
which he never got from you or from
me."

"Granting that he is great at twenty-
five," said Mrs. Perkins, after a few moments' reflection, "is that such a horrible
thing ?"

"It isn't for the parents of the successful youth, but for the successful youth
himself it's something awful," returned
Thaddeus, with a convincing shake of the
head. "If no one ever lived beyond the
age of thirty-five it wouldn't be so bad,
but think of living to be even so young
as sixty, with a big reputation to sustain
through more than half of that period ! I
wouldn't want to have to sustain a big name
for twenty-five years. Success entails conspicuousness, and conspicuousness makes
error almost a crime. Put your mind on
it for a moment. Think of Teddy here.
How nervous it would make him in everything he undertook to feel that the eyes
of the world were upon him. And take

into consideration that other peculiarity
of human nature which leads us all, you
and me as well as every one else, to believe that the man who does not progress
is going backward, that there is no such
thing as standing still; then think of a
man illustrious enough for seventy at
twenty-five—at the limit of success, with
all those years before him, and no progress possible! No, my dear. Don't let's
talk of school for Teddy yet."

"I am sure I don't want to force him,"
said Mrs. Perkins, "but it sometimes
seems to me that he needs lessons in discipline. I can't be following around
after him all the time, and it seems to
me some days that I do nothing but find
fault with him. I don't want him to
think I'm a stern mother; and when he
tells me, as he did yesterday, that he
wishes I'd take a vacation for a month, I
can't blame him."

"Did he tell you that?" asked Thaddeus, with a chuckle.

"Yes, he did," replied Mrs. Perkins.

"I'd kept him in a chair for an hour because he would tease Tommy, and when finally I let him go I told him that he was wearing me out with his naughtiness. About an hour later he came back and said, 'You have an awful hard time bringin' me up, don't you?' I said yes, and added that he might spare me the necessity of scolding him so often, to which he replied that he'd try, but thought it would be better if I'd take a vacation for a month. He hadn't much hope for his own improvement."

Thaddeus shook internally.

"He's perfectly wild, too, at times," Mrs. Perkins continued. "He wants to do such fearful things. I caught him sliding down the banisters yesterday headforemost, and you know how he was at the Mountain House all summer long. Perfectly irrepressible."

"That's very true," said Thaddeus. "I was speaking of it to the doctor up there, and asked him what he thought I'd better do."

"And what did he say?" asked Mrs. Perkins.

"He stated his firm belief that there was nothing you or I could do to get him down to a basis, but thought Hagenbeck might accomplish something."

"No doubt he thought that," cried Bessie. "No doubt everybody thought that, but it wasn't entirely Teddy's fault. If there is anything in the world that is well calculated to demoralize an active-minded, able-bodied child, it is hotel life. Teddy was egged on to all sorts of indiscretions by everybody in the hotel, from the bell-boys up. If he'd stand on his head on the cashier's desk, the cashier would laugh first, and then, to get rid of him, would suggest that he go into the dining-room and play with the head-waiter; and when he upset the contents of his bait-box in Mrs. Harkaway's lap, she interfered when I scolded him, and said she liked it. What can you do when people talk that way?"

"Get him to upset his bait-box in her

lap again," said Thaddeus. "I think if he had been encouraged to do that as a regular thing, every morning for a week, she'd have changed her tune."

"Well, it all goes to prove one thing," said Mrs. Perkins, "and that is, Teddy needs more care than we can give him personally. We are too lenient. Whenever you start in to punish him it ends up with a game; when I do it, and he says something funny, as he always does, I have to laugh."

"How about the ounce-of-prevention idea?" suggested Thaddeus. "We've let him go without a nurse for a year now—why can't we employ a maid to look after him—not to boss him, but to keep an eye on him—to advise him, and, in case he declines to accept the advice, to communicate with us at once? All he needs is directed occupation. As he is at present, he directs his own occupation, with the result that the things he does are of an impossible sort."

"That means another servant for me to manage," sighed Mrs. Perkins.

"True; but a servant is easier to manage than Teddy. You can discharge a servant if she becomes impossible. We've got Teddy for keeps," said Thaddeus.

"Very well—so be it," said Mrs. Perkins. "You are right, I guess, about school. He ought not to be forced, and I'd be worried about him all the time he was away, anyhow."

So it was decided that Teddy should have a nurse, and for a day or two the subject was dropped. Later on Mrs. Perkins reopened it.

"I've been thinking all day about Teddy's nurse, Thaddeus," she said, one evening after dinner. "I think it would be nice if we got him a French nurse. Then he could learn French without any forcing."

"Good scheme," said Thaddeus. "I approve of that. We might learn a little French from her ourselves, too."

"That's what I thought," said Bessie; and that point was decided. The new nurse was to be French, and the happy

parents drew beatific visions of the ease
with which they should some day cope
with Parisian hotel-keepers and others in
that longed-for period when they should
find themselves able, financially, to visit
the French capital.

But—

Ah! Those buts that come into our
lives! Conjunctions they are called! Are
they not rather terminals? Are they not
the forerunners of chaos in the best-laid
plans of mankind? If for every "but"
that destroys our plan of action there were
ready always some better-succeeding plan,
then might their conjunctive force seem
more potent; as life goes, however, unhap-
pily, they are not always so provided, and
the English "but" takes on its Gallic significance, which leads the Frenchman to
define it as meaning "the end."

There was an object-lesson in store for
the Perkinses.

On the Sunday following the discussion with which this story opens, the Perkinses, always hospitable, though distinct-

ly unsociable so far as the returning of
visits went, received a visit from their
friends the Bradleys. Ordinarily a visit
from one's town friends is no very great
undertaking for a suburban host or hostess, but when the town friends have children from whom they are inseparable, and
those children have nurses who, whither-
soever the children go, go there also, such
a visit takes on proportions the stupen-
dousness of which I, being myself a suburban entertainer, would prefer not to dis-
cuss, fearing lest some of my friends with
families, recalling these words, might consider my remarks of a personal nature.
Let me be content with saying, therefore,
that when the Bradleys, Mr. and Mrs.,
plus Master and Miss, plus Harriet, the
English nurse, came to visit the Perkins
homestead that Sunday, it was a momen-
tous occasion for the host and hostess,
and, furthermore, like many another mo-
mentous occasion, was far-reaching in its
results.

In short, it provided the Perkins fam-

ily with that object-lesson to which I have
already alluded.

The Bradleys arrived on Sunday night,
and as they came late little Harry Bradley and the still smaller Jennie Bradley
were tired, and hence not at all respon-
sive to the welcomes of the Perkinses,
large or small. They were excessively
reticent. When Mrs. Perkins, kneeling before Master Harry, asked him the wholly
unnecessary question, " Why, is this Harry ?" he refused wholly to reply ; nor could
the diminutive Jennie be induced to say
anything but " Yumps " in response to a
similar question put to her, " Yumps "
being, it is to be presumed, a juvenilism
for " Yes, ma'am." Hence it was that
the object-lesson did not begin to develop.
until breakfast on Sunday morning. The
first step in the lesson was taken at that
important meal, when Master Harry observed, in stentorian yet sweetly soprano
tones :

" Hi wants a glarse o' milk."

To which his nurse, standing behind

his chair to relieve the Perkinses' maid of
the necessity of looking after the Bradley
hopefuls, replied :

" 'Ush, 'Arry, 'ush ! Wite till yer
arsked."

Mrs. Bradley nodded approval to Harriet, and observed quietly to Mrs. Perkins
that Harriet was such a treasure ; she
kept the children so well in subjection.

The incident passed without making
any impression upon the minds of any
but Thaddeus junior, who, taking his cue
from Harry, vociferously asserted that he,
too, wished a glass of milk, and in such
terms as made the assertion tantamount
to an ultimatum.

Then Miss Jennie seemed to think it
was her turn.

" Hi doan't care fer stike. Hi wants
chickin," said she. " I'n't there goin' ter
be no kikes ?"

Mrs. Perkins laughed, though I strong-
ly suspect that Thaddeus junior would
have been sent from the table had he vent-
ured to express a similar sentiment. Mrs.

Bradley blushed ; Bradley looked severe ;
Perkins had that expression which all
parents have when other people's children are involved, and which implies the
thought, "If you were mine there'd be
trouble; but since you are not mine, how
cunning you are !" But Harriet, the
nurse, met the problem. She said :

"Popper's goin' ter have stike, Jinnie;
m'yby Mr. Perkins 'll give yer lots o'
gryvy. Hit i'n't time fer the kikes."

Perhaps I ought to say to those who
have not studied dialect as "she is spoke"
that the word m'yby is the Seven Dials
idiom for maybe, itself more or less
an Americanism, signifying "perhaps,"
while "kikes" is a controvertible term
for cakes.

After breakfast, as a matter of course,
the senior members of both families at-
tended divine service, then came dinner,
and after dinner the usual matching of
the children began. The hopefuls of
Perkins were matched against the scions
of Bradley. All four were brought down-

stairs and into the parental presence in
the library.

"Your Harry is a fine fellow, Mrs.
Bradley," said Thaddeus.

"Yes, we think Harry is a very nice
boy," returned Mrs. Bradley, with a fond
glance at the youth.

"Wot djer si about me, mar ?" asked
Harry.

"Nothing, dear," replied Mrs. Bradley,
raising her eyebrows reprovingly.

"Yes, yer did, too," retorted Harry.
"Yer said as 'ow hi were a good boy."

"Well, 'e i'n't, then," interjected Jennie. "'E's a bloomin' mean un. 'E took
a knoife an' cut open me doll."

"'Ush, Jinnie, 'ush !" put in the nurse.
"Don't yer tell tiles on 'Arry. 'E didn't
mean ter 'urt yer doll. 'Twas a haxident."

"No, 'twasn't a haxident," said Jennie. "'E done it a-purpice."

"Well, wot if hi did ?" retorted Harry.
"Didn't yer pull the tile off me rockin'-
'orse ?"

"Well, never mind," said Bradley, seeing how strained things were getting. "Don't quarrel about it now. It's all done and gone, and I dare say you were both a little to blame."

"'Hi war'n't!" said Harry, and then the subject was dropped. The children romped in and out through the library and halls for some time, and the Bradleys and Perkinses compared notes on various points of interest to both. After a while they again reverted to the subject of their children.

"Does Harry go to school?" asked Bessie.

"No, we think he's too young yet," returned Mrs. Bradley. "He learns a little of something every day from Harriet, who is really a very superior girl. She is a good servant. She hasn't been in this country very long, and is English to the core, as you've probably noticed, not only in her way of comporting herself, but in her accent."

"Yes, I've observed it," said Bessie. "What does she teach him?"

"Oh, she tells him stories that are more or less instructive, and she reads to him. She's taught him one or two pretty little songs — ballads, you know — too. Harry has a sweet little voice. Harry, dear, won't you sing that song about Mrs. Henry Hawkins for mamma?"

"Don't warn'ter," said Harry. "Hi'm sick o' that bloomin' old song."

"Seems to me I've heard it," said Thaddeus. "As I remember it, Harry, it was very pretty."

"It is," said Bradley. "It's the one you mean—'Oh, 'Lizer! dear 'Lizer! Mrs. 'Ennery 'Awkins.' Harry sings it well, too; but I say, Thad, you ought to hear the nurse sing it. It's great."

"I should think it might be."

"She has the accent down fine, you know."

"Sort of born to it, eh?"

"Yes; you can't cultivate that accent and get it just right."

"I'll do 'Dear Old Dutch' for yer,"

suggested Harry. " Hi likes thet better 'n
' Mrs. 'Awkins.' "

So Harry deserted "Mrs. 'Awkins" and
sang that other pathetic coster - ballad,
" Dear Old Dutch," and, to the credit of
Harriet, the nurse, it must be said that
he was marvellously well instructed. It
could not have been done better had the
small vocalist been the own son of a London coster-monger instead of the scion of
an American family of refinement.

Thus the day passed. Jennie proved
herself quite as proficient in the dialect
of Seven Dials as was Harry, or even
Harriet, and when she consented to stand
on a chair and recite a few nursery
rhymes, there was not an unnoticed " h "
that she did not, sooner or later, pick up
and attach to some other word to which
it was not related, as she went along.

In short, as far as their speech was concerned, thanks to association with Harriet, Jennie and Harry were as perfect little cockneys as ever ignored an aspirate.

The visit of the Bradleys, like all other

things, came to an end, and Bessie, Thaddeus, and the children were once more left to themselves. Teddy junior, it was observed, after his day with Harry, developed a slight tendency to misplace the letter " h " in his conversation, but it was soon corrected, and things ran smoothly as of yore. Only—the Only being the natural sequence of the But referred to some time since—Mr. and Mrs. Perkins changed their minds about the French nurse, and it came about in this way :

"Thaddeus," said Bessie, after the Bradleys had departed, " what is the tile of a rockin'-'orse ?"

" I don't know. Why ?" asked Thaddeus.

" Why, don't you remember," she said, " young Harry Bradley accused Jennie of pulling out the tile of his rockin'-'orse ?"

" Oh yes ! Ha, ha !" laughed Thaddeus. "So she did. I know now. Tile is cockney for tail."

" Did you notice the accent those children had ?"

"Yes."

"All got from the nurse, too ?"

"True."

"Ah, Teddy, what do you think of our getting a French maid, after all ? Don't you think that we'd run a great risk ?"

"Of what ?"

"Of having Ted speak—er—cockney French."

"H'm—yes. Very likely," said Thaddeus. "I'd thought of that myself, and, I guess, perhaps we'd better stick to Irish."

"So do I. We can correct any tendency to a brogue, don't you think ?"

"Certainly," said Thaddeus. "Or, if we couldn't, it wouldn't be fatal to the boy's prospects. It might even help him if he—"

"Help him ? If what ?"

"If he ever went into politics," said Perkins.

And that was the object-lesson which a kindly fate gave to the Perkinses in time to prevent their engaging a French maid for the children.

As to its value as a lesson, as to the value of its results, those who are familiar with French as spoken by nurse-instructed youths can best judge.

I am not unduly familiar with that or any other kind of. French, but I have ideas in the matter.

THE CHRISTMAS GIFTS OF
THADDEUS

THE CHRISTMAS GIFTS OF
THADDEUS

THAT you may thoroughly comprehend
how it happened that on last Christmas
Day Thaddeus meted out gifts of value so
unprecedented to the domestics of what
he has come to call his " menagerie "—
the term menage having seemed to him
totally inadequate to express the state of
affairs in his household—I must go back
to the beginning of last autumn, and nar-
rate a few of the incidents that took place
between that period and the season of
Peace on Earth and Good-will to Men.
Should I not do so there would be many,
I doubt not, who would deem Thaddeus's
course unjustifiable, especially when we
are all agreed that Christmas Day should

be for all sorts and conditions of men the
gladdest, happiest day of all the year.

Thaddeus and Bessie and the little
Thad had returned to their attractive
home after an absence of two months in
a section of the Adirondacks whither the
march of civilization had not carried such
comforts as gas, good beds, and other luxuries, to which the little family had become so accustomed that real camp-life,
with its beds of balsam, lights of tallow,
and "fried coffee," possessed no charms
for them. They were all renewed in spirit and quite ready to embark once more
upon the troubled seas of house-keeping;
and, as they saw it on that first night at
home, their crew was a most excellent
one. The cook rose almost to the exalted
level of a chef in the estimation of Thaddeus as course upon course, to the number of seven, each made up of some deli-
cacy of the season, came to the table and
received the indorsement which comes
from total consumption. They were well
served, too, these courses; and the two

heads of the family, when Mary, the waitress, would enter the butler's pantry, leaving them alone and unobserved, nodded
their satisfaction to each other across the
snow-white cloth, and by means of certain
well-established signals, such as shaking
their own hands and winking the left
eye simultaneously, with an almost vicious
jerk of the head, silently congratulated
themselves upon the prospects of a peace-
ful future in a domestic sense.

"That was just the best dinner I have
had in centuries," said Thaddeus, as they
adjourned to the library after the meal
was over. "The broiled chicken was so
good, Bess, that for a moment I wished
I were a bachelor again, so that I could
have it all; and after I got over my first
feeling of hesitation over the oysters, and
realized that it was September with an R
—belated, it is true, but still there—and
ate six of them, I think I could have gone
down - stairs and given cook a diamond
ring with seven solitaires in it and a re-
ceipted bill for a seal-skin sacque. I don't

see how we ever could have thought of discharging her last June, do you ?"

"It was a good dinner," said Bessie, discreetly ignoring the allusion to their intentions in June ; for she had a well-defined recollection that at that time Bridget had given signs of emotional insanity every time she was asked to prepare a five-o'clock breakfast for Thaddeus and his friends, to the number of six, who had acquired the habit of going off on little shooting trips every Saturday, making the home of Thaddeus their headquarters over Sunday, when the game the huntsmen had bagged the day before had to be plucked, cleaned, and cooked by her own hands for dinner. "And it was nicely selected, too," she added. " I sometimes think that I'll let Bridget do the ordering at the market."

" H'm ! Well," said Thaddeus, shaking his head dubiously, "I haven't a doubt that Bridget could do it, and would be very glad to do it ; but I don't believe in setting a cook up in business."

" How do you mean ?"

" I mean that I haven't any doubt that Bridget would in a very short time become a highly successful produce-broker with bull tendencies. The chicken market would be buoyant, and the quotations on the Stock Exchange of, say, B., S., and P.-U.-C.—otherwise, Beef, Succotash, and Picked-Up-Codfish — would rise to the highest point in years. Why, my dear, by Christmas-time cook would have our surplus in her own pocket-book ; and in the place of the customary five oranges and an apple she would receive from the butcher a Christmas-card in the shape of a check of massive, if not graceful, proportions. No, Bess, I think the old way is the best."

" Perhaps it is. By-the-way, John has kept the grounds looking well, hasn't he ? The lawn doesn't seem to have a weed on it," said Bessie, walking to the window and gazing out at the soft velvety sward in the glow of twilight.

" Yes, it looks pretty well ; but there's

a small heap of stuff over there near the fence which rather inclines me to believe that the weeds have been pulled out within the last few days—in fact, since you wrote to announce our return. John is an energetic man in an emergency, and I haven't a doubt he has been here at least once a week ever since we left. I'll keep a record of John this fall."

And so the two contented home-comers talked happily along, and when they closed their eyes in sleep that night they were, upon the whole, very well satisfied with life.

Weeks elapsed, and with them some of the air-castles collapsed. Whether custom staled the infinite variety of the cook's virtues, and age withered the efficiency of Mary, the waitress, or whether something was really and radically wrong with the girls, Thaddeus and Bessie could not make out. Certain it was, however, that by slow degrees the satisfaction for which that first dinner seemed to stand as guarantor wore away, and dissatisfaction entered the household. Mary developed a fondness for church at most inconvenient hours—hours at which, in fact, neither Thaddeus nor Bessie had ever supposed church could be. That it was eternal they both knew, but they had always supposed there were intermissions. Then the cook's family, which had hitherto been moderately healthful, began to show signs of invalidism, though no such calamity as actual dissolution ever set its devastating step within the charmed circle of her relatives. Cousins fell ill whom she alone could comfort; nephews developed maladies for which she alone could care; and, according to Thaddeus's record, John had been compelled on penalty of a fine to attend the funerals of some twenty-four deceased intimate friends in less than two months, although the newspapers contained no mention of the existence of a possible epidemic in the Celtic quarter. It is true that John showed a more pronounced desire to make his absence less inconvenient to his

employer than did Mary and the cook,
by providing a substitute when the Ancient Order of Funereal Hibernians compelled him to desert the post of duty; but
Thaddeus declared the "remedy worse
than the disease," for the reason that
John's substitute—his own brother-in-
law—was a weaver by trade, whose bas-
kets the public did not appreciate, and
whose manner of cutting grass in the
early fall and of tending furnace later on
was atrocious.

"If I could hire that man in summer,"
Thaddeus remarked one night when
John's substitute had "fixed" the furnace so that the library resembled a cold-
storage room, "I think we could make
this house an arctic paradise. He seems
to have a genius for taking warmth by the
neck and shaking enough degrees of heat
out of it to turn a conflagration into an
iceberg. I think I'll tell the Fire Com-
missioners about him."

"He can't compare with John," was
Bessie's answer to this.

"No. I think that's why John sends him here when he is off riding in carriages in honor of his deceased chums. By the side of Dennis, John is a jewel."

"John is very faithful with the furnace," said Bessie. "He never lets it go down. Why, day before yesterday I turned off every register in the house, and even then had to open all the windows to keep from suffocating."

"But that wasn't all John, my dear," said Thaddeus. "The Weather Bureau had something to do with it. It was a warm day for this season of the year, anyhow. If John could combine the two businesses of selling coal and feeding furnaces, I think he would become a millionaire. And, by-the-way, I think you ought to speak to him, Bess, about the windows. Since you gave him the work of window-cleaning to do, it is evident that he thinks I have nothing to say in the matter, for he persistently ignores my requests that he clean them in squares as they are made, and not rub up a little

circle in the middle, so that they look
like blocks of opalescent glass with plate-
glass bulls'-eyes let into the centre. Look
at them now."

" Dennis did that. John had to go to
Mount Vernon with his militia company
to-day."

"Ah! Dennis is well named, for his
name is— But never mind. I'll credit
John with his twelfth day off in four
weeks."

From John to Bridget, in the matter
of days off, was an easy step, though such
was Bessie's consummate diplomacy that
Thaddeus would probably have continued in ignorance of the extent to which
Bridget absented herself had they not
both taken occasion one day to visit some
relatives in Philadelphia, and on their
return home at night found no dinner
awaiting them.

"What's the matter now?" asked Thaddeus, a little crossly, perhaps, for visiting
relatives in Philadelphia invariably irri-
tated him—possibly because he and they

did not agree in politics, and their assumption that Thaddeus's party was entirely made up of the ignorant and self-seeking was galling to him. "Why isn't dinner ready?"

"Mary says that an hour after we left cook got a telegram from New York saying that her brother was dying, and she had to go right off."

"I thought that brother was dying last week?"

"No; that was her mother's brother. He got well. This is another person entirely."

"Naturally," snapped Thaddeus. "But next time we get a cook let's have one whose relatives are all dead, or in the old country, where they can't be reached. I'm tired of this business."

"Well, you shouldn't be cross with me about it, Thad," said Bessie, with a teary look in her eyes. "I have to put up with a great deal more of it than you have, only you never know of it. Why, I've cooked one-half of my own luncheons in the last month."

"And the dinners, too, I'll wager," growled Thaddeus.

"No; she's always got home for dinner heretofore."

"Well, we'll keep a record-book for her, too, then. And we'll be generous with her. We'll allow her just as I was allowed in college—twenty-five per cent. in cuts. If she has twenty-five and a fifth per cent. she goes."

"I don't think I understand," said Bessie.

"Well, we'll put it this way : There are thirty days in a month. That means ninety meals a month. If she cooks sixty-seven and a half of them she can stay; if she fails to cook the other twenty-two and a half she can stay ; but woe be unto her if she slips up by even so little as a millionth part of the sixty-eighth !"

"I don't see how you can manage the half part of it."

"We'll leave that to her," said Thaddeus, firmly ; "and, what is more, we'll put John and Mary on the same basis,

and Dennis we won't have on any basis at
all. A man who will take advantage of
his brother's absence at a wake to black
the shoes of that brother's only employer
with stove-polish is not the kind of a man
I want to have around."

"It will be a very good plan," said
Bessie, "for all except Mary. Her ab-
sences she cannot well avoid. She has to
go to church."

"How many times a week does she
have to go ?" queried Thaddeus.

"She is required to go to confession."

"Well, let her reform, and then she'll
have nothing to go to confession for. I
don't believe that's where she goes, either.
I notice that one-half those evenings she
takes off, permitting me to mind the front
door, and enabling us both to acquire
proficiency in the art of helping ourselves
at dinner, there's a fireman's ball or a
policeman's hop or a letter-carriers' theatre party going on somewhere in the
county, and it's my belief the worship-
ping she does on these occasions is at the

shrine of Terpsichore or that of Melpom-
ene, which is a heathen custom and not
to be tolerated here. If she's so fond of
living in church we can quote to her
Hamlet's advice to Ophelia—'Get thee
to a nunnery!' Why, Bess, I was morti-
fied to death the other night when Bradley dined here. He's all the time brag-
ging about his menagerie, and I tried to
bluff him out and make him believe we
were waited on by angels in disguise, and
you know what happened. He came,
saw, and I was regularly knocked out.
You let us in; we waited on ourselves;
cook had prepared the seven-o'clock dinner at five to give her a chance to go to
the hospital to see her brother-in-law
with the measles; John had one of his
Central-African fires on, and Bradley's
laughing about it yet."

"Mr. Bradley was very disagreeable
the other night, anyhow," sniffed Bessie. "He acted as if he were camping
out!"

"Well, I can't honestly say I blame him

for that," retorted Thaddeus. "It only
needed a balsam bed and a hole in the
roof to let the rain in on him to complete the illusion."

Finally, December came, and the tendencies of absenteeism on the part of the
servants showed no signs of abatement.
They were remonstrated with, but it made
no difference. They didn't go out, they
declared, because they wanted to, but because they had to. Cook couldn't let her
relatives go unattended. Mary's religious
scruples simply dragged her out of the
house, try as she would to stay in; and as
for John, as long as Dennis was on hand
to take his place he couldn't see why
Mr. Perkins was dissatisfied. To tell the
truth, John had recently imbibed some
more or less capitalistic—or anticapital-
istic—doctrines, and he was quite inca-
pable of understanding why, if a street-
contractor, for instance, was permitted
by the laws of the land to sublet the
work for which he had contracted, he,
John, should not be permitted to sub-

let his contract to Dennis, piecemeal,
or even as a whole, if he saw fit to
do so.

Thaddeus, seeing that Bessie was very
much upset by the condition of affairs,
had said little about it since Thanksgiv-
ing Day, when he had said about as much
as the subject warranted after a six-
course dinner had been hurried through
in one hour, two courses having been
omitted that Bridget might catch the
train leaving for New York at 3.10. Nor
would he have said anything further than
the final words of dismissal had he not
come home late one afternoon to dress
for a dinner at his club, when he discovered that, owing to the usual causes, the
week's wash, which the combined efforts
of cook and waitress should have finished
that day, was delayed twenty-four hours,
the consequence being that Thaddeus had
to telephone to the haberdashery for a
dress-shirt and collar.

"It's bad enough having one's wife buy
these things for one, but when it comes

to having a salesman sell you over a telephone the style of shirt and collar 'he
always wears himself,' it is maddening,"
began Thaddeus, and then he went on
at such an outrageous rate that Bessie
became hysterical, and Thaddeus's con-
science would not permit of his going out
at all that night, and that was the beginning of the end.

"I'll fix 'em at Christmas-time," said
Thaddeus.

"You won't forget them at Christmas,
I hope, Thad," said Bessie, whose forgiving nature would not hear of anything so
ungenerous as forgetting the servants during the holidays.

"No," laughed Thaddeus. "I won't
forget 'em. I'll give 'em all the very
things they like best."

"Oh, I see," smiled Bessie. "On the
coals-of-fire principle. Well, I shouldn't
wonder but it would work admirably.
Perhaps they'll be so ashamed they'll do
better."

"Perhaps—if the coals do not burn too

deep," said Thaddeus, with a significant smile.

Christmas Eve arrived, and little Thad's tree was dressed, the gifts were arranged beneath it, and all seemed in readiness for the dawning of the festal day, when Bessie, taking a mental inventory of the packages and discovering nothing among them for the servants save her own usual contribution of a dress and a pair of gloves for each, turned and said to Thaddeus :

" Where are the hot coals ?"

" The what ?" asked Thaddeus.

" The coals of fire for the girls and John."

" Oh !" Thaddeus replied, " I have 'em in the library. I don't think they'll go well with the tree."

" What are they ?" queried Bess, with a natural show of curiosity. " Checks ?"

" Yes, partly," said Thaddeus. "Mary is to have a check for $16, Bridget one for $18, and John one for $40."

" Why, Thaddeus, that's extravagant.

Now, my dear, there's no use of your doing anything of that—"

"Wait and see," said Thaddeus.

"But, Teddy!" Bessie remonstrated. "Those are the amounts of their wages. You will spoil them, and if I—"

"As I said before, wait, Bess, wait!" said Thaddeus, calmly. "You'll understand the whole scheme to-morrow, after breakfast."

And she did, and when she did she almost wished for a moment that she didn't, for after breakfast Thaddeus summoned the three offenders into his presence, and the effect was not altogether free from painful features to the forgiving Bess.

"Bridget," Thaddeus said, "do you remember what Mrs. Perkins gave you last Christmas?"

"I do not!" replied Bridget, rather uncompromisingly; for it was a matter of history that she thought Mrs. Perkins on the last Christmas festival had shown signs of parsimony in giving her a calico gown instead of one of silk.

"Well, you won't forget next year what you got this," said Thaddeus, dryly. "Here is an envelope containing $18, the amount of your wages until January 1st. Mary, what did you get last Christmas?"

"A box of candy, sir."

"Nothing else?"

"I believe there was a dress of some kind. I gave it to my cousin."

"Good. I am glad you were so generous. Here is an envelope for you. It has $16 in it, your wages up to January 1st."

Bessie stood in the door-way, a mute witness to what seemed to her an incomprehensible scene.

"John, what did you get?"

"Foive dollars an' a day off."

"And a two-dollar bill for Dennis, eh?"

"Dennis got that."

"True. Well, John, here's $40 for you —that pays you until January 1st. Now, it strikes me that, considering the behavior of you three people, I am very generous to pay you your wages a week in advance, but I am not going to stop there. I have studied you all very carefully, and I've tried to discover what it is you are fondest of. Cook and Mary do not seem to care much for dresses, though I believe there are dresses and gloves under the tree for them, which fact they will doubtless forget by next Christmas Day. The five dollars and a day off John seems to remember, though from his manner of recalling it I do not think his remembrance is a very pleasing one. Now I've found out what it is you all like the best, and I'm going to give it to you."

Here the trio endeavored to appear gracious, though they were manifestly uneasy and a bit dissatisfied with what John would have called " the luks of t'ings."

"Cook, from the 1st of January, may go to her relatives, and stay until they're every one of them restored to health, if it takes forty years. Mary may consider herself presented with sixty years' vacation without pay ; and for you, John, I

have written this letter of recommenda-
tion to the proprietors of a large undertaking establishment in New York, who
will, I trust, engage you as a chief mourn-
er, or perhaps hearse-driver, for the balance of your days.   At any rate, you, too,
after January 1st, may consider yourself
free to go to any funeral or militia exer-
cises, or anything else you may choose to
honor with your presence, at your own ex-
pense.   You are all given leave of absence
without pay until further notice.   I wish
you a merry Christmas.   Good-morning."

There were no farewells in the house
that day; and inasmuch as there was no
Christmas dinner either, Thaddeus and
Bessie did not miss the service of the
waitress, who, when last seen, was walking airily off towards the station, accompanied by the indignant John and a bun-
dle-laden cook.   Next day their trunks
went also.

"It was rather a hard thing to do on
Christmas Day, Thaddeus," said Bessie,
a little later.

"Oh no," quibbled Thaddeus. "It was very easy under the circumstances, and quite appropriate. This is the time of peace on earth and good-will to men. The only way for us to have peace on earth was to get rid of those two women; and as for John, he has my good-will, now that he is no longer in my employ."

A STRANGE BANQUET

A STRANGE BANQUET

"THADDEUS," said Bessie to her husband as they sat at breakfast one morning, shortly after the royal banquet over which "Grimmins" had presided, "did you hear anything strange in the house last night? Something like a footstep in the hall?"

"No," said Thaddeus. "I slept like a top last night. I didn't hear anything. Did you?"

"I thought so," said Bessie. "About two o'clock I waked up with a start, and while it may have been a sort of waking dream, I was almost certain I heard a rustling sound out in the hall, and immediately after a creaking on the stairs, as though there was somebody there."

"Well, why on earth didn't you wake

me, Bess?" returned Thaddeus. "I
could easily have decided the matter by
getting up and investigating."

"That was why I didn't wake you, Teddy. I'd a great deal rather lose the silver
or anything else in the house a burglar
might want than have you hit on the head
with a sand-club," said Bessie. "You
men are too brave."

"Thank you," said Thaddeus, with a
smile, as he thought of a certain discussion he had had not long before at the
club, in which he and several other brave
men had reached the unanimous conclusion that the best thing to do at dead of
night, with burglars in the house, was
to crawl down under the bedclothes and
snore as loudly as possible. "Neverthe-
less, my dear, you should have told me."

"I will next time," said Bessie.

"Was anything in the house disturbed?" Thaddeus asked.

"No," said Bessie. "Not a thing, as
far as I can find out. Mary says that
everything was all right when she came

down, and the cook apparently found things straight, because she hasn't said anything."

So Thaddeus and Bessie made up their minds that the latter had been dreaming, and that nothing was wrong. Two or three days later, however, they changed their minds on the subject. There was something decidedly wrong, but what it was they could not discover. They were both awakened by a rustling sound in the hallway, outside of their room, and this time there was a creak on the stairs that was unmistakable.

"Don't move, Thaddeus," said Bessie, in a terrified whisper, as Thaddeus made a brave effort to get up and personally investigate. "I wouldn't have you hurt for all the world, and there isn't a thing down-stairs they can take that we can't afford to lose."

Thaddeus felt very much as Bessie did, and it would have pleased him much better to lie quietly where he was than run the risk of an encounter with thieves.

He had been brave enough in the company of men to advocate cowardice in an emergency of just this sort, but now that this same course was advocated by his wife, he saw it in a different light. Prudence was possible, cowardice was not. He must get up, and get up he did; but before going out of his room he secured his revolver, which had lain untouched and unloaded in his bureau-drawer for two years, and then advanced cautiously to the head of the stairs and listened— Bessie meanwhile having buried her face in her pillow as a possible means of assuaging her fears. It is singular what a soothing effect a soft feather pillow sometimes has upon the agitated nerves if the nose of the agitated person is thrust far enough into its yielding surface.

"Who is there?" cried Thaddeus, standing at the head of the stairs, his knees all of a shake, but whether from fear or from cold, as an admirer of Thaddeus I prefer not to state.

Apparently the stage-whisper in whioh

this challenge to a possible burglar was
uttered rendered it unavailing, for there
was no reply ; but that there was some
one below who could reply Thaddeus was
now convinced, for there were sounds in
the library — sounds, however, suggestive
of undue attention to domestic duties
rather than of that which fate has map-
ped out for house-breakers. The library
floor was apparently being swept.

"That's the biggest idiot of a burglar
I've ever heard of," said Thaddeus, returning to his room.

"Wh-wha-what, d-dud-dear?" mum-
bled Mrs. Perkins, burying her ear in the
pillow for comfort now that she was compelled to take her nose away so that she
might talk intelligibly.

"I say that burglar must be an idiot,"
repeated Thaddeus. "What do you suppose he is doing now?"

"Wh-wha-what, d-dud-dear?" asked
Bessie, apparently unable to think of any
formula other than this in speaking, since
this was the second time she had used it.

" He is sweeping the library."

" Then you must not go down," cried
Bessie, sitting up, and losing her fear for
a moment in her anxiety for her husband's safety. "A burglar you might
manage, but a maniac—"

" I must go, Bess," said Thaddeus,
firmly.

" Then I'm going with you," said Mrs.
Perkins, with equal firmness.

" Now, Bess, don't be foolish," returned Thaddeus, his face assuming a graver
expression than his wife had ever seen
there. "This is my work, and it is none
of yours. I positively forbid you to stir
out of this room. I shall be very careful,
and you need have no concern for me. I
shall go down the backstairs and around
by the porch, and peep in through the library window first. The moonlight will
be sufficient to enable me to see all that
is necessary."

" Very well," acquiesced Bessie, "only
do be careful."

Thaddeus donned his long bath-robe,

put on his slippers, and started to de-
scend. The stairs were so dark that he
could with difficulty proceed—and perhaps it was just as well for Thaddeus
that they were. If there had been light
enough for him to see two great glaring
eyes that stared at him through that
darkness out from the passageway at the
foot of the stairs, upon which he turned
his back when he went out upon the
porch, it is not unlikely that a very serious climax to his strange experience
would have been reached then and there.
As it was, he saw nothing, but kept
straight ahead, stepped noiselessly out
upon the piazza, crept stealthily along
in the soft light of the moon, until he
reached the library window. There he
stopped and listened. All was still within—so still that the beating of his heart
seemed like the hammering of a sledge
upon an anvil by contrast. Then, raising himself cautiously upon his toes, he
peered through the window into the room,
the greater part of which was made visi-

ble by the wealth of the moon's light
streaming into it.

"Humph!" said Thaddeus, after he
had directed his searching gaze into every corner. "There isn't anybody there
at all. Most incomprehensible thing I
ever heard of."

Rising, he walked back to the piazza
door, and went thence boldly into the
library and lit the gas. His piazza obser-
vations were then verified, for the room
was devoid of life, save for Thaddeus's
own presence; but upon the floor before
the hearth was a broom, and there were
evidences also that the sweeping sounds
he had heard had been caused by no less
an instrument than this, for in the corner
of the fireplace was a heap of dust, cigar
ashes, and scraps of paper, which Thaddeus remembered had been upon the
hearth in greater or less quantity when he
had turned out the gas to retire a few
hours before.

"This is a serious matter," he said to
himself. "Something is wrong, and I

doubt if there have been burglars in the house; but I can ascertain that without trouble. If the doors and windows are all secure the trouble is internal."

Every accessible door and window on the basement and first floor was examined, and, with the exception of the piazza door, which Thaddeus remembered to have unlocked himself a few minutes before, every lock was fastened. The disturbance had come from within.

"And Bess must never know it," said he; "it would worry her to death." And then came a thought to Thaddeus's mind that almost stopped the beating of his heart. "Unless she has discovered it in my absence," he gasped. In an instant he was mounting the stairs to hasten to Bessie's side, as though some terrible thing were pursuing him.

"Well, what was it, Ted?" she asked, as he entered the room.

Perkins gave a sigh of relief. All was safe enough above-stairs at least.

"Nothing much," said Thaddeus, in a moment. "There is no one below."

"But what could it have been?"

"I haven't the slightest idea," said Thaddeus, "unless it was a stray cat in the house. The sweeping sound may have been caused by a cat scratching its collar—or purring—or—or—something. At any rate, things appear to be all right, my dear, so let's go to sleep."

Thaddeus's assumed confidence in the rightness of everything, rather than his explanations, was convincing to Mrs. Perkins, and in a very short while she was sleeping the sleep of the just and serene; but to Thaddeus's eye there came no more sleep that night, and when morning came he rose unrefreshed. There were two problems confronting him. The first was to solve the mystery of the swept library floor; the second was to do this without arousing his wife's suspicions that anything was wrong. To do the first he deemed it necessary to remain at home that day, which was easy, for Thaddeus was more or less independent of office-work.

"I'm glad you're not going down," said Mrs. Perkins, when he announced his intention of remaining at home. "You will be able to make up for your loss of sleep last night."

"Yes," said Thaddeus. "It's the only thing I can do, I'm so played out."

Breakfast passed off pleasantly in spite of a great drawback — the steak was burned almost to a crisp, and the fried potatoes were like chips of wood.

"Margaret seems to be unfamiliar with the art of cooking this morning," said Thaddeus.

"So it would seem," said Bessie. "This steak is horrible."

"The worst part of it is," said Thaddeus, "she has erred on the wrong side. If the steak were underdone it wouldn't be so bad. Isn't it a pity Edison can't invent a machine to rarefy an overdone steak?"

"That would be a fine idea," smiled

Bessie. "And to take a Saratoga chip and make it less like a chip off a granite block."

"I don't mind the potatoes so much," said Thaddeus. "I can break them up in a bowl of milk and secure a gastronomic novelty that, suitably seasoned, isn't at all bad, but the steak is hopeless."

"Maybe she heard that cat last night, and thought it was a burglar, just as we did," Bessie suggested. "I can't account for a breakfast like this in any other way, can you?"

"No," said Thaddeus, shortly, and then he had an idea; and when Thaddeus had an idea he was apt to become extremely reticent.

"Poor Thad!" thought Bessie, as she noted his sudden change of demeanor. "He can't stand loss of sleep."

The morning was spent by Thaddeus in the "noble pastime of snooping," as he called it. The house was searched by him in a casual sort of way from top to bottom for a clew to the mystery, but without avail. Several times he went below to the

cellar, ostensibly to inspect his coal sup-
ply, really to observe the demeanor of
Margaret, the cook. Barring an unusual pallor upon her cheek, she appeared to
be as she always had been ; but with the
waitress it was different. Mary was evidently excited over something, but over
what Thaddeus could not, of course, de-
termine at that time. Later in the day,
however, the cause of her perturbation
came out, and Thaddeus's effort to keep
Bessie from anxiety over the occurrence
of the night before was rendered unavailing. It was at luncheon. The table was
set in a most peculiar fashion. The only
china upon it was from an old set which
had been discarded a year previous to the
time of this story, and Bessie naturally
wanted to know why, and the waitress
broke down.

"It's — it's all we have, ma'am," said
she, her eyes filling with tears.

"All we have ?" echoed Mrs. Perkins in
surprise. "Why, what do you mean ?
Where is the other set ?"

"I don't know," protested the waitress.

"You don't know?" said Thaddeus, taking the matter in hand. "Why don't you know? Isn't the china a part of your care?"

"Yes, sir," replied the maid, "but—it's gone, sir, and I don't know where."

"When did you miss it?" asked Thaddeus.

"Not until I came to set the table for lunch."

"Was it in its proper place at breakfast-time?"

"I didn't notice, sir. The breakfast dishes were all there, but I don't remember seeing the other plates. I didn't think to look."

"Then it wasn't a cat," said Bessie, sinking back into her chair; "we have been robbed."

"Well, it's the first time on record, I guess, that thieves have ever robbed a man of his china," said Thaddeus, calmly. "Have you looked for the plates?" he added, addressing the waitress.

"No, sir," she replied, simply. "Where could I look?"

"That's so — where?" said Bessie. "There isn't much use looking for dishes when they disappear like that. They aren't like whisk-brooms or button-hooks to be mislaid easily. We have been robbed; that's all there is about that."

"Oh, well," said Thaddeus, "let's eat lunch, and see about it afterwards."

This was quite easy to say, but to eat under the circumstances was too much for either of the young householders. The luncheon left the table practically un-touched; and when it was over Thad-deus called his man into the house, wrote a note to the police-station, asking for an officer in citizen's clothes at once, and despatched it by him, with the injunc-tion to let very little grass grow under his feet on the way down to headquarters. He then summoned the waitress into the library.

"Have you said anything to Margaret about the china?" he asked.

"Yes, sir," she replied.

"What did you say ?"

"I told her as how wasn't it funny the way it had went, sir."

"And what did she say ?"

"Nothing, sir. Only she seemed to think it was funny, because she laughed."

"And what did you say then ?"

"Nothing, Mr. Perkins. Margaret and me have very little conversation, because she don't fancy me, and prefers talkin' to herself like."

"H'm !" said Thaddeus. "Talks to herself, does she ?"

"All the time, sir," returned the waitress, "and she seems very fond of it, sir. She laughs, and says things, and then laughs again. She does it by the hour."

"How long has this been going on ?"

"About a week, sir. I noticed it first last time I had my day out. I didn't get in until nearly eleven o'clock, and I found her sitting at the table havin' supper and talkin' and laughin' like as though there was folks around."

"She was entirely alone, was she?" asked Thaddeus.

"Yes, sir."

"What did you do when you came in?"

"I said 'Hello' to her and sat down opposite to her at the table, where there was a place set, and I told her I was glad she had something to eat and a place set for me, because I hadn't had any supper and I was hungry, sir."

"Did she make any reply?"

"No, sir. She looked at me kind of indignant, and turned out the gas and went up to bed, leavin' me in the dark."

Thaddeus's brow grew thoughtful again. It wrinkled into a half-dozen lines as he asked:

"Why didn't you speak of this before?"

"It ain't for me to be telling tales, Mr. Perkins," she said. "All cooks as I've lived with is queer like, and I didn't think any more about it."

"All right," said Thaddeus. "You may go. Only, Mary, don't speak of the plates

again to Margaret. Say as little to her
as you can, in fact, about anything. If
you notice anything queer, report to me
at once."

The waitress left the room, and Thaddeus turned to his desk. It was plain
from his appearance that light was beginning to be let in on places that up to this
point had been more or less dark to him,
although, as a matter of fact, he could
not in any way account for the mystery
of the vanished plates any more than he
could for the sweeping of the library in
the still hours of the night. He had an
idea as to who the culprit was, and what
that idea was is plain enough to us, but
the question of motive was the great
puzzle to him now.

"If she did take them, why should
she ?" was the problem he was trying to
solve ; and then, as if his trials were not
already great enough for one day, Bessie
broke excitedly into the room.

"Thaddeus !" she cried, "there's something wrong in this house ; my best table-

cloth is missing, our dessert-spoons are gone, and what do you suppose has happened ?"

"I don't know—a volcano has developed in the cellar, I suppose," said Thaddeus.

"No," said Bessie, "it isn't as bad as that; but the ice-cream man has telephoned up to know whether we want the cream for dinner or for eleven o'clock, according to the order as he understands it."

"Well," said Thaddeus, "I don't see anything very unusual in an ice-cream man's needing to be told three or four times what is expected of him."

"But I never ordered any cream at all," said Bessie.

"Ah," said Thaddeus, "that's different. Did you tell Partinelli so ?"

"I did, and he said he was sure he wasn't mistaken, because he had taken the order himself."

"From you ?"

"No, from Margaret."

"Then it's all right," said Thaddeus; "it's a clew that fits very nicely into my theory of our recent household disturbances. If you will wait, I think things will begin to develop very shortly, and then we shall be able to dismiss this indictment against the cat we thought we heard last night."

"Do you think Margaret is dishonest?"

"I don't know," said Thaddeus. "I shouldn't be surprised if she had friends with taking ways; in other words, my dear, I suspect that Margaret is in league with people outside of this house who profit by her mistaken notions as to how to be generous; but I can't prove it yet."

"But what are you going to do?"

"Set a watch. I have sent for a detective," said Thaddeus.

This was too much for Bessie. She was simply overcome, and she sat squarely down upon the arm-chair, which fortunately was immediately behind her. I think that if it had not been, she would have plumped down upon the floor.

"Detective !" she gasped.

"Exactly," said Thaddeus, "and here he comes," he added, as a carriage was driven up to the door and one of the citizen police descended therefrom.

"You would better leave us to talk over this matter together," said Thaddeus, as he hastened to the door. "We shall be able to manage it entirely, and the details might make you nervous."

"I couldn't be more nervous than I am," said Bessie; "but I'll leave you just the same."

Whereupon she went to her room, and Thaddeus, for an hour, was closeted with the detective, to whom he detailed the whole story.

"It's one of the two," said the latter, when Thaddeus had finished, "and I agree with you it is more likely to be the cook than the waitress. If it was the waitress, she couldn't have stood your examination as well as you say she did. Perhaps I'd better see her, though, and talk to her myself."

"No, I shouldn't," said Thaddeus; "we'll pass you off as a business acquaintance of mine up from town, and you can stay all night and watch developments."

So it was arranged. The detective was introduced into the family as a correspondent of Thaddeus's firm, and he settled down to watch the household. Afternoon and evening went by without developments, and at about eleven o'clock every light in the house was extinguished, and the whole family, from the head of the house to the cook, had apparently retired.

At half-past eleven, however, there were decided signs of life within the walls of Thaddeus's home. The clew was working satisfactorily, and the complete revelation of the mystery was close at hand.

The remainder of the narrative can best be told in the words of the detective:

"When Mr. Perkins sent for me," he said, "and told me all that had happened, I made up my mind that he had a servant in his house for whom the police had been

on the lookout for some time. I thought
she was a certain Ellen Malony, alias
Bridget O'Shaughnessy, alias many other
names, who was nothing more nor less
than the agent of a clever band of thieves
who had lifted thousands of dollars of
swag in the line of household silver, valu-
able books, diamonds, and other things
from private houses, where she had been
employed in various capacities. I could
not understand why she should have made
'way with the dishes and Mrs. Perkins's
table-cloth, but there's no accounting for
tastes of people in that line of business,
so I didn't bother much trying to reason
that matter out.

" After we'd had dinner and spent the
evening in Mr. Perkins's library, the family went to bed, and I pretended to do the
same. Instead of really going to bed, I
waited my chance and slipped down the
stairs into the dining-room, and got under
the table. At eleven o'clock the maid-
servants went up to their rooms, and at
quarter-past there wasn't a light burning

in the house. I sat there in the dining-
room waiting, and just as the clock struck
half-past eleven I heard a noise out on
the stairs, and in less than half a minute a sulphur match was struck almost
over my head under the table, and there
stood the cook, her face livid as that of
a dead person, and in her hand she held
a candle, which she lit with the match.
From where I was I could see everything
she did, which was not much. She simply gathered up all the table fixings she
could, and started down-stairs into the
kitchen with 'em. Then I went up to
Mr. Perkins's room and called him. He
put on his clothes and got out his revolver,
when we stole down-stairs together, leaving Mrs. Perkins up-stairs, with her boy's
nurse and the waitress to keep her company.

"In a second we were in the laundry,
which was as dark as the ace of spades,
except where the light from four gas-jets
in the kitchen streamed in through the
half-open door. Mr. Perkins was for

pouncing in on the cook at once, but I
was after the rest of the gang as much as
I was for the cook, and I persuaded him
to wait ; and, by thunder, we were paid
for waiting. It was the queerest case I
ever had.

"That woman—looking for all the world
like a creature from some other part of the
universe than this earth, her eyes burning like two huge coals, her cheeks as
yellow and clear as so much wax, and her
lips blue-white, with a great flaming red
tongue sort of laid between them—worked
like a slave cleaning the floor, polishing
the range, and scrubbing the table. Then
she dusted all tho chairs, and, produc-
ing the missing table-cloth, she laid it
snow-white upon the table. In two minutes more the lost china was brought to
light out of the flour-barrel, polished off,
and set upon the table—enough for twenty
people. The dining-room things I had
seen her take she arranged as tastefully as
any one could want, and then the finest
lay-out in the way of salads, cakes, fruits,

and other good things I ever saw was brought in from the cellar. To do all this took a marvellously short time. It was five minutes of midnight when she got through, and then she devoted three minutes to looking after herself. She whisked out a small hand-glass and touched up her hair a bit. Then she washed her hands and pinned some roses on her dress, smiled a smile I can never forget in my life, and opened the kitchen door and went out.

"'She's going to give a supper!' whispered Mr. Perkins.

"'It looks like it,' said I. 'And a mighty fine one at that.'

"In a minute she came back with a pail, in which were four bottles of champagne, in her hand. This she took into the cellar, returning to the kitchen as the clock struck twelve.

"Then the queerest part began," said the detective. "For ten minutes by the clock people were apparently arriving, though, as far as Mr. Perkins or I could

see, there wasn't a soul in the kitchen besides Margaret.   She was talking away
like one possessed.   Every once in a
while she'd stop in the middle of a sentence and rush to the door and shake
hands with some, to us invisible, arrival.
Then she'd walk in with them, chatting
and laughing.   Several times she went
through the motion of taking people's
hats, and finally, if we could judge from
her actions, she had 'em all seated at the
table.   She passed salads all around, helping each guest herself.   She sent them
fruit and cakes, and then she brought out
the wine, which she distributed in the
same fashion.   She also apologized because some ice - cream she had ordered
hadn't come.

"When the invisible guests appeared
to have had all they could eat, she began
the chatty part again, and never seemed
to be disturbed but once, when she requested some one not to sing so loud for
fear of disturbing the family.

"Altogether it was the weirdest and

rummest thing I'd ever seen in my life.
We watched it for one full hour, and then
we quit because she did. At one o'clock
she apparently bade her guests good-
night, after which she gathered up and
put away all the eatables there were left
—and, of course, everything but what she
had eaten herself still remained—cleaned
all the dishes, restored them to their
proper places in the dining-room pantry,
and went back up-stairs to her room.

"Mr. Perkins and I didn't know what
to make of it. There wasn't a thing
stolen, and it was clear to my mind that
I'd done the woman an injustice in con-
necting her with thieves. She was honest, except in so far as she had ordered
all those salads and creams and things
from time to time on Mr. Perkins's account, which was easy enough for her to
do, since Mrs. Perkins let her do the
ordering. There was only one explana-
tion of the matter. She was crazy, and I
said so.

"'I fancy you are right,' said Mr. Perkins. 'We'll have to send her to an asylum!'

" 'That's the thing,' said I, 'and we'd better do it the first thing in the morning. I wouldn't tackle her to-night, because she's probably excited, and like as not would make a great deal of trouble.'

" And that," said the detective, " was where Mr. Perkins and I made our mistake. Next morning she wasn't to be found, and to this day I haven't heard a word of her. She disappeared just like that," he said, snapping his fingers. " Of course, I don't mean to say that anything supernatural occurred. She simply must have slipped down and out while we were asleep. The front door was wide open in the morning, and a woman answering to her description was seen to leave the Park station, five miles from the Perkins house, on the six-thirty train that morning."

" And you have no idea where she is now?" I asked of the detective, when he had finished.

"No," he answered, "not the slightest. For all I know she may be cooking for you at this very minute."

With which comforting remark he left me.

For my part, I hope the detective was wrong. If I thought there was a possibility of Margaret's ever being queen of my culinary department, I should either give up house-keeping at once and join some simple community where every man is his own chef, or dine forevermore on canned goods.

JANE

JANE

SHE was quite the reverse of beautiful
—to some she was positively unpleasant
to look upon; but that made no difference to Mrs. Thaddeus Perkins, who, after long experience with domestics, had
come to judge of the value of a servant
by her performance rather than by her
appearance. The girl—if girl she were,
for she might have been thirty or sixty,
so far as any one could judge from a
merely superficial glance at her face and
figure—was neat of aspect, and, what was
more, she had come well recommended.
She bore upon her face every evidence
of respectability and character, as well as
one or two lines which might have indicated years or toothache—it was difficult
to decide which. On certain days, when

the weather was very warm and she had
much to do, the impression was that the
lines meant years, and many of them,
accentuated as they were by her pallor,
the whiteness of her face making the
lines seem almost black in their intensi-
ty. When she smiled, however, which
she rarely did — she was solemn enough
to have been a butler—one was impressed
with the idea of hours of pain from a
wicked tooth. At any rate, she was engaged as waitress, and put in charge of
the first floor of the Perkins household.

"I fancy we've at last got a real treasure," said Mrs. Perkins. "There's no
nonsense about Jane—I think." The last
two words were added apologetically.

"Where did you get her?" asked Thaddeus. "At an Imbecility Office?"

"I don't quite know what you mean—
an Imbecility Office?"

"Only my pet, private, and particular
name for it, my dear. You would speak
of it as an Intelligence Office, no doubt,"
was the reply. "My observation of the

fruit of Intelligence Offices has convinced
me that they deal in Imbecility."

"Not quite," laughed Mrs. Perkins.
"They look after Domestic Vacancies."

"Well, they do it with a vengeance,"
said Perkins. "We've had more vacancies in this house to do our cooking and
our laundering and our house-work generally than two able-bodied men could
shake sticks at. It seems to me that the
domestic servant of to-day is fonder of
preoccupation than of occupation."

"Jane, I think, is different from the
general run," said Mrs. Perkins. "As I
said, she has no nonsense about her."

"Is she — ah — an ornament to the
scene—pretty, and all that?" asked Perkins.

"Quite the reverse," replied the little
house-keeper. "She is as plain as a—as
a—"

"Say hedge-fence and be done with
it," said Perkins. "I'm glad of it. What's
the use of providing a good dinner for
your friends if they are going to spend

all their time looking at the waitress ?
When I give a dinner it makes me tired
to have the men afterwards speak of the
waitress rather than of the *purée* or the
birds. If any domestic is to dominate
the repast at all it should be the cook."

"Service counts for a great deal, though,
Ted," suggested Mrs. Perkins.

"True," replied Thaddeus; "but on
the whole, when I am starving, give me a
filet béarnaise served by a sailor, rather
than an empty plate brought in in style
by a butler of illustrious lineage and im-
pressive manner." Then he added : "I
hope she isn't too homely, Bess—not a
'clock-stopper,' as the saying is. You
don't want people's appetites taken away
when you've worked for hours on a menu
calculated to tickle the palates of your
guests. Would her homeliness—ah—efface itself, for instance, in the presence
of a culinary creation, or is it likely to
overshadow everything with its inefface-
able completeness ?"

"I think she'll do," returned Mrs. Per-

kins ; "especially with your friends, who,
it seems to me, would one and all insist
upon finishing a 'creation,' as you call
it, even if lightning should strike the
house."

"From that point of view," said he,
"I'm confident that Jane will do."

So Jane came, and for a year, strange
to relate, was all that her references
claimed for her. She was neat, clean,
and capable. She was sober and industrious. The wine had never been better
served; the dinner had rarely come to the
table so hot. Had she been a butler of
the first magnitude she could not so have
discouraged the idea of acquaintance ;
her attraction, if anything, was a combi-
nation of her self-effacement and her ug-
liness. The latter might have been noticed as she entered the dining-room ; it
was soon forgotten in the unconsciously
observed ease with which she went through
her work.

"She's fine," said Perkins, after a dinner of twelve covers served by Jane with

a pantry assistant. "I've always had a sneaking notion that nothing short of a butler could satisfy me, but now I think otherwise. Jane is perfection, and there is nothing paralyzing about her, as there is about most of those reduced swells who wait on tables nowadays."

In August the family departed for the mountains, and the house was left in charge of Jane and the cook, and right faithfully did they fulfil the requirements of their stewardship. The return in September found the house cleaned from top to bottom. The hardwood floors and stairs shone as they had rarely shone before, and as only an unlimited application of what is vulgarly termed "elbow-grease" could make them shine. The linen was immaculate. Ireland is not freer from snakes than was the house of Perkins from cobwebs, and no speck of dust except those on the travellers was visible. It was evident that even in the absence of the family Jane was true to her ideals, and the heart of Mrs. Perkins was glad. Further-

more, Jane had acquired a full third set
of teeth, which seemed to take some of
the lines from her face, and, as Perkins
observed, added materially to the general
effect of the surroundings, although they
were distressingly new. But, alas! they
marked the beginning of the end. Jane
ceased to wait upon the table with that
solemnity which is essential to the manner of a "treasure"; she smiled occasionally, and where hitherto she had treated
the conversation at the table with stolid
indifference, a witticism would invariably
now bring the new teeth into view.

"Alas!" cried Thaddeus, "our butleress
has evoluted backwards. She grins like
an ordinary waitress."

It was too true. The possession of brill-
iantly white teeth seemed to have brought
with it a desire to show them, which was
destructive of that dignity with which
Jane had previously been hedged about,
and substituted for it a less desirable atmosphere of possible familiarity, which
might grow upon very slight provocation

into intimacy, not to mention a nearer approach to social equality.

"I don't suppose we can blame her exactly," said Perkins, when discussing one or two of Jane's lapses from her old-time standard. "I haven't a doubt that if I'd gone for years without teeth, I'd become a regular Cheshire cat, with a new, complete *édition de luxe* of celluloid molars. Still, I wish she'd paid more attention to the dinner and less to Mr. Barlow's conversation last night. She stood a whole minute, with the salad-bowl in her hand, waiting for him to reach the point of his story about the plumber who put a gas-pipe through Shakespeare's tenor in Westminster Abbey, and when he finished, and she smiled, you'd have thought a dozen gravestones to the deceased's memory had been conjured up before us."

"It's a small fault, Thaddeus," returned Mrs. Perkins, "but I'll speak to her about it."

"Oh, I wouldn't," said Perkins; "let it go; she means well, and when we got

her we didn't suspect she'd turn out such
a jewel. She's merely approaching her
norm, that is all. We ought to be thank-
ful to have had such perfection for one
year. It's too bad it couldn't continue ;
but what perfection does ?"

Nothing, therefore, was said, and Jane
smiled on, yet waited most acceptably and
kept all things decently and in order—for
a little while. Along about Christmas-
time a further decadence and additional
flaw in the jewel was discovered, and it
was Perkins himself who discovered it.
It happened one day while he was at work
alone in the house, Mrs. Perkins having
gone out shopping. A friend from Boston
appeared—a friend interested in bric-à-
brac and china generally. Thaddeus, to
whom a luncheon in solitary grandeur
was little short of abomination, invited
his Boston friend to stay and share pot-
luck with him, knowing, hypocrite that
he was, that pot-luck did not mean pot-
luck at all, but a course luncheon which
many men would have found all-sufficient

at dinner. The Boston friend accepted,
and the luncheon was served by Jane. In
the course of the repast the visitor observed :

"Pretty good china you have, Perkins."

"Yes," returned Thaddeus, "pretty
good. I've always had a *penchant* for
china. My mother-in-law thinks I'm extravagant, and sometimes I think she is
right. You never saw my Capodimonte
coffees, did you ?"

"No," replied the Bostonian, "I never
did. Where'd you get 'em ?"

"London," replied Perkins, "last time
I was over. You must see them, by all
means. Ah, Jane, hand Mr. Bunkerrill
one of the Capodimonte coffees."

"Wan o' the what, sorr ?" asked the
treasure.

Thaddeus blushed. To have his jewel
go back on him at such a crisis was excessively annoying. "One of those gold
after-dinner coffee-cups—one of the little
ones, with the flowery raised figures," he
said, sharply.

"Oh!" said Jane, "wan o' thim with somebody else's initial on the bottom?"

"Yes," said Thaddeus, fuming inwardly.

"Quite a connoisseur, that woman," laughed the visitor, as Jane went after the dinner-cup. "She's observed the china mark. She know's N doesn't stand for Perkins."

Thaddeus laughed weakly. "She probably thinks we got them second-hand," he said.

"Very likely you did," retorted the Bostonian, and Jane returned with the desired cup. "An admirable specimen," continued the connoisseur; and then, turning the cup bottom upwards in search of the mark, he disclosed to his own and Thaddeus's astonished gaze no less an object than the remains of a mashed green pea, a reminiscence of the last Perkins dinner, and conclusive evidence that at times Jane was not as careful in the washing of her china as she might have been.

It would be futile and useless for me to

attempt to describe the emotions of Thaddeus. I fancy a large enough number of us have been through similar experiences to comprehend the man's mortification and his inward wrath. It was too great to find suitable expression at the moment. Nothing short of the absolute destruction of the cup and the annihilation of Jane could have adequately expressed Perkins's true feelings. He was not by nature, however, a scene-maker—it would have been better if he had been—so he said nothing, abiding by his rule, which seemed to be that the man of the house would do better to reprehend the shortcomings of a delinquent servant by blowing up his wife rather than by going direct to the core of the trouble and reading the maid a lecture. A great many men adopt this same method. I do. It is the easiest, though it is possibly prompted by that cowardice which is latent within us all. I never in my life have discharged more than one servant, and I not only did not do it gracefully, but discharged the wrong one ; since which time I have left all that sort of work to others more competent than I. Perkins's method was precisely this.

"I'm not going to interfere," was his invariable remark in cases of the kind under discussion ; which was unwise, for if he had ever scolded a servant as he did his wife for the servant's fault he might have secured better service sooner or later.

Unfortunately, when Mrs. Perkins reached home that night she was so very tired with her exertions in the shops that Thaddeus hadn't the heart to tell her what had happened, and when morning came the episode was forgotten. When it did recur to his mind it so happened that Mrs. Perkins was out of reach. The result was that a month had passed before Mrs. Perkins came into possession of the facts, and it was then, of course, too late to mention it to Jane.

"You should have given her a good talking to at the time," said Mrs. Perkins. "It's awful ! I don't know what has got into Jane. My best table-cloth has got a great hole in it, and she is very careless with the silver. My fruit-knife last night was not clean."

"I suppose *you* spoke to her about that?" said Perkins, smiling.

"Not exactly; I sent for another, and handed her the dirty one," returned Mrs. Perkins. "I guess she felt all that I could have said."

And time went on, and Jane continued to decay. She pulled corks from olive-bottles with the carving-fork prongs and bent them backwards. She developed a habit of going out and leaving her work undone. The powdered sugar was allowed to resolve itself into small, hard, pill-shaped lumps of various sizes. Breakfast had a way of being served cold. The coffee was at times merely tepid; in short, it seemed as if she really ought to be discharged; but then there was invariably some reason for postponing the fatal hour. Either her kindness to the children or a week or two of the old-time efficiency, her

unyielding civility, her scrupulous hon-
esty, her willing acquiescence in any new
duty imposed, an impression that she was
suffering, any one or all of these reasons
kept her on in her place until she became
so much a fixture in the household, so
much one of the family, that the idea of
getting rid of her seemed beyond the possibility of realization. That the axe should
fall her employers knew well, and many a
resolve was taken that at the end of the
season she should go, yet neither Mrs.
Perkins nor her husband liked to tell her
so.   Her good points were still too potent, although none could deny that all
confidence in her efficiency was shattered
past repair. The situation finally reached
a point where it inspired reflections of a
more or less humorous order.

"I tell you what I think," said Thaddeus one evening, after a particularly fla-
grant breach on Jane's part, involving a
streak of cranberry sauce across a suppos-
ititiously clean plate: "you won't discharge her, Bess, and I won't; suppose

we send for Mr. Burke, and get him to do
it."

Mr. Burke was the one reliable man in
town. It didn't make much difference
what the Perkinses wanted done, they
generally sent for Mr. Burke to do it,
largely because when he attempted a com-
mission he saw it through. A carpenter
and builder by trade, he had for many
years looked after the repairs needful to
the Perkins dwelling; he had come often
between Thaddeus and unskilled labor;
he had made bookcases which were dreams
of convenience and sufficiently pleasing to
the eye; he had "fixed up" Mrs. Perkins's garden; he had supplied the family
with a new gardener when the old one
had taken on habits of drink, which de-
stroyed not only himself but the cab-
bages; he had kept an eye on the plumb-
ers; he had put up, taken down, and
repaired awnings — in short, as Perkins
said, he was a "Universal." Once, when
a delicate piece of bric-à-brac had been
broken and the china-mender asserted

that it could not be mended, Perkins had
said, "See if Burke can't fix it," and
Burke had fixed it ; and as final tribute
to this wonder, Perkins had said, in suf-
ering :

"My dear, I'm afraid I have appendi-
citis. Send for Mr. Burke."

" Mr. Burke !" echoed his wife.

" Yes, Mr. Burke," moaned the sufferer.
" If my vermiform appendix is to be re-
moved, I'd rather have Mr. Burke do it
with a chisel and saw than any surgeon I
know ; and I won't take ether either, because it is such a satisfaction to see him
work."

So, when this happy pair of householders had reached what might be de-
scribed as the grand climacteric of their
patience, and it was finally decided that
Jane's usefulness was a thing of the past,
and utterly beyond redemption, Thaddeus
naturally suggested turning to his faithful friend, Mr. Burke, to rid them of their
woes, and, indeed, but for Jane's own in-
tervention, I fear that course would have

proved the sole alternative to her becoming an irremovable fixture in the household.   But it was Jane herself who solved the problem.

It was two days after the cranberry episode that the solution came, and it was in this wise :

"Did ye send for me ?" Jane asked, suddenly materializing in Mrs. Perkins's room.

"No, Jane, I haven't ; why ?"

The girl began to shed tears.

"Because—you'd ought to have, ma'am. I know woll enough that I ain't satisfactory to you," she returned, her voice quivering, "and I can't be, and I know you want me to go—and I—I've come to give you notice."

Then Mrs. Perkins looked at Jane with sorrow on her countenance, for she had acquired an affection for her which the maid's delinquencies had not been able to efface.

"Can't you try and do better ?" she asked.

"No, ma'am," returned Jane. "Not with the system—never. Mr. Perkins is too easy, and you do be so soft-hearted it don't keep a girl up to her work. When I first come here, ma'am, not knowin' ye well, I was afraid to be anything but what was right, but the way you took accidents, and a bit of a shortcomin' once in a while, sort of took away my fear, and I've been goin' down hill ever since. Servant-girls is only human, Mrs. Perkins."

Mrs. Perkins looked at Jane inquiringly.

"We needs to be kept up to our work just as much as anybody else, and when a lady like yourself is too easy, it gets a girl into bad habits, and occasionally it does us good if the gentleman of the house will swear at us, Mrs. Perkins, and sort of scare us, so it does. It was that that was the makin' of me. The last place I was in, ma'am, I was so afraid of both the missus and the gentleman that I didn't dare to be careless; and I didn't dare be careless with you until I found you all the

time a-smilin', whatever went wrong, and
Mr. Perkins never sayin' a word, whether
the dishes come to the table clean or not."

"Well, Jane," said Mrs. Perkins, somewhat carried away by this course of rea-
soning, "you haven't been what we hoped
—there is no denying that; but knowing that you were disappointing us, why
couldn't you have made a special effort?"

"Oh, Mrs. Perkins," sobbed the poor
woman, "you don't understand. We're
all disappointin' to them we loves, but—
it's them we fear—"

"Then why aren't you afraid of us?"

Jane laughed through her tears. The
idea was preposterous.

"Afraid of you and Mr. Perkins?
Ah!" she said, sadly, "if I only could be—
but I can't. Why, Mrs. Perkins, if Mr.
Perkins should come in here now and
swear at me the way Mr. Barley did when
I worked there, I'd know he was only
puttin' it on, and that inside he'd be
laughin' at me. No, ma'am, it's no use.
I feel that I must go, or I'll be forever

ruined. It was the cranberry showed me; a girl had ought to be discharged for that. Dirty dinner plates isn't excusable, and yet neither of you said a word, and next week it 'll be the same way—so I'm goin'. You won't send me off, so I've got to do it myself."

"Very well, Jane," said Mrs. Perkins; "if that is the way you feel about it we'll have to part, I suppose. I am sorry, but—"

The sentence was not finished, for Jane rushed weeping from the room, and within a few days, her place having been filled, the house knew her no more, except as an occasional visitor, ostensibly to see the children. Later she got a place to her satisfaction, and one night the Perkinses were invited to dine with Jane's new employers. They went and found their old-time "butler" at the very zenith of her powers. She served the dinner as she had never served one in her palmiest days in the Perkins's dining-room; and when all was over, and when Mrs. Perkins went up-stairs to don her wrap to return home, she found Jane above waiting to help her.

"I am glad to see you so happy, Jane," she said, as the girl held her cloak.

"Ah, ma'am, I'm not very happy."

"You ought to be, here. Your work to-night was perfect."

"Yes," said Jane, "it had to be, for" —here her voice fell to a whisper—"I don't dare let it be different, ma'am. Mrs. Harkins is a regular divvle, and the ould gentleman — well, ma'am, he do swear finer 'n any gentleman I ever met. It's just the place for me."

And Jane sighed as her old mistress left her.

"Wasn't she great, Bess?" said Thaddeus, on the way home.

"She was, indeed," replied Mrs. Perkins, with a smile. "It's a pity I'm not a divvle."

Thaddeus laughed. "That's so," he said; "or that I never learned to swear like a gentleman, eh?"

THE END

Reprint Publishing

FOR PEOPLE WHO GO FOR ORIGINALS.

This book is a facsimile reprint of the original edition. The term refers to the facsimile with an original in size and design exactly matching simulation as photographic or scanned reproduction.

Facsimile editions offer us the chance to join in the library of historical, cultural and scientific history of mankind, and to rediscover.

The books of the facsimile edition may have marks, notations and other marginalia and pages with errors contained in the original volume. These traces of the past refers to the historical journey that has covered the book.

ISBN 978-3-95940-056-5

www.reprintpublishing.com

www.ingramcontent.com/pod-product-compliance
Lightning Source LLC
Chambersburg PA
CBHW051132020726
47501CB00005B/1476